Looking for God

Within the Kingdom of Religious Confusion

AW Schade

Foreword by SANKARA SARANAM

AnotherView Publishing

. HUDSON, FLORIDA

To my friends: Brian and Carolyn. Here is the reverses story! and equal Jesus are given willing, promise. Love Art

AW Schade

Printed in the United States, by RJ Communications

ISBN (paperback)   0-9788565-0-3

Library of Congress Control Number 2006907212

Special Notes

The names in this book are fictional and no name or reference to any person or position is intended to represent any individual, past, present or future. While the story of the journey is fiction, the book contains factual references which the reader can validate through historical text, if desired.

Throughout the story I have used "God" in the masculine form, as referenced in most religious texts. Whether God is male or female, black or white, or encompasses all human virtues is immaterial to this writing. God as a man is the common, acceptable reference and the one I have used to keep this writing simple.

Also, the name God, as used by the Jewish and Christian faiths, is synonymous with Allah, of the Islamic faith. I will reference both in capital letters to demonstrate respect for the same Supreme Being. At times, the names may be interchanged. No disrespect is intended.

In Gratitude

To my family and friends: for their support and encouragement.

To Sankara Saranam, who selflessly provided advice, to this stranger

AW Schade

Looking for God

AW Schade

FOREWORD

As we cross the threshold of the twenty first century, many of those who have chosen to believe in God within the patronage of the three monotheistic faiths of Judaism, Christianity and Islam have not had the luxury of spending years researching the history of their religion. Often, this has inhibited tolerance toward different faiths, and reinforced an unwillingness to ask penetrating questions about God. While many believers may not admit to being confused, confusion is freely available to all who decide to question accepted doctrine.

At the same time, questions concerning how the world works, with an appreciation for the vastness of the universe, are more common and poignant today than when the world first heard of the Hebrews. We have made steady progress in material science despite the discomfort it can cause the true believer, and our ability to historically analyze past events repeatedly challenges long held beliefs.

Despite our commonplace reliance on reason and logic to function properly in our daily lives, and the growing necessity to short circuit our intellectual faculties in order maintain faith, religious obsession remains consistently used as a means to promote public support for ethnic hatred and wars fought to secure material wealth, and to impose religious beliefs on others. These contradictions of modern life clarify how failing trust in our social institutions outwardly reflects inner spiritual uncertainty.

Widespread vulnerability of the self has resulted in a shift toward extreme religious ideology for a segment of the populace. Emboldened by an Evangelical Christian president, religious America is in the throws of civil unrest where not merely the age of the earth is called into question, but America's secular roots are also a major point of contention. As the so-called biblical "End Times" are seriously anticipated by tens of millions of people, science and religion clash on the field of policy making and unabashed contempt for opposing points of view is standard fare on television and talk radio.

It is in these times that Schade is publishing the book you hold in your hand. Art's rare gift to his reader is not one of theoretical conjecture, but in his sincerity to simplify the chaos plaguing the kingdom of religion. In this work of fiction, the simple but real truths that philosophers spend years contemplating are humbly presented through the journey of his characters' search to find God. Though limiting his story to Western traditions, Art arrives at universal truths which are as pertinent today to human beings as they were throughout all other periods of history.

In limiting the scope to traditions commonly associated with the West, however, Art in fact does a service to readers who are, by conditioning, inclined to limit their search for answers about God to the three monotheistic religions. This book serves as both a bridge to nonfiction works which discuss religion in greater depth and as a map out of the confusion Western religions have wrought in the name God.

Like most authors who want the best for their books, Art could have labored over this book without end, even for years, to create a spotless novel. However, as I reviewed one version after the other, I found that the original spontaneity and innocence of discovery was being eclipsed by descriptive narrative.

By returning to his conversational style of writing, Art served the reader best by not overwriting his book and maintaining its natural honesty and innocence. Knowing Art, the only award he is interested in is the reward of peace for his readers, a peace he has clearly found in his search for God.

Sankara Saranam; 2006
Author of "God Without Religion"
The Pranayama Institute

AW Schade

AGONY

Jacob fell to his knees, weeping, as he watched his nine-year-old daughter, Jessica, lowered into the abyss of death, a site eloquently referred to earlier in the sermon as her "final resting place." Jacob never considered it her final resting place. To him, it was the cold, dark hole where Jessica's body would remain alone forever.

"I should have protected you!" Jacob muttered repeatedly, as family and friends stood by helplessly, unable to comfort him, trying to control their own agony as they watched the descending coffin.

Protect her? Jacob thought. Unlike he did when he saw the car speed through the stop sign, striking Jessica as she walked her bicycle across the road, through the unspoken safety of the crosswalk. He yelled to her to stop when he saw the car racing towards her, but she was too far away to hear him. As always, when she spotted him, she enthusiastically smiled and waved to her daddy, never seeing the approaching instrument of death.

As he ran towards her, screaming at her to stop, he watched in horror as the car sped through the stop sign, hitting Jessica, hurling her body and bicycle into the air. Then, as if time had altered his senses, he watched her fall upon the asphalt road, seemingly in slow motion.

"Where is God?" he screamed, as he cradled her lifeless body in his arms. "Where is God?" he demanded! It was the same demand he had shouted decades before on the battlefields of Vietnam, when he held the dead or mutilated bodies of brother Marines. "Where is God?" he repeated, not expecting an answer.

Clutching Jessica against his chest he suddenly heard a voice behind him, a stranger hoping to comfort Jacob, said, "She is with God." Surprised by the voice, Jacob turned toward the man and shouted uncharacteristically, "How the hell do you know she is with God? Why did God take her in the first place; she should be with me!" The man ignored Jacob's response, bent down and wrapped his arms around Jacob and Jessica, and began to cry. He held them until the ambulance arrived.

At Jessica's memorial service, Jacob A. Hinsen felt the agony of self-condemnation, demanding of himself answers to why he did not do more to prevent her death. He chastised himself as he told those around him that he should have run faster to catch her before her body hit the asphalt; yelled louder, warning her of the danger of the approaching vehicle; or begged God sooner to take him instead of Jessica.

The well-intended condolences after the services did nothing to heal the anguish in his heart. Nor, did they lessen the scorn he felt as his thoughts reluctantly drifted to Jessica's mother Brenda, who was absent from her daughters funeral, as she had been during Jessica's short life.

Brenda was a beautiful young woman with long reddish hair and a smile as broad and bright as the Cheshire Cat's. She was intelligent, well educated, and a successful lawyer, like Jacob, but not the "mothering type." Jacob met her at a legal seminar in New York City. He was forty years old and fell in love at first glance. It took Brenda, then only thirty-two, several months before she told him that she thought she loved him too.

During their two-year courtship, sex and alcohol kept them together in a lifestyle of convenience, which satisfied both their short-term needs for fun and loving companionship. All was going well until one drunken evening they conceived Jessica.

Jacob was ecstatic when Brenda told him the news of her pregnancy, but she did not share his enthusiasm. She told him she was too young, and did not want to be held down by a baby.

Nevertheless, after a few weeks of relentless arguments and pleas from Jacob, she decided to marry him and have their baby.

Their eleven-month marriage was tumultuous, to say the least. Nevertheless, Jacob sobered up after his daughter's birth, and his new aspiration was to be the best father he could be for Jessica. Brenda, however, was not ready for motherhood, nor interested in remaining his wife. She refused to change her lifestyle, and they divorced when Jessica was two months old. Brenda willingly granted full custody of the baby to Jacob.

Soon after the divorce, Jacob heard Brenda was promoted to a new position as an international legal attaché. Global assignments, enjoying the good life he assumed.

Throughout her young life, he recalled Jessica only asked a few times about her mother's whereabouts. He always answered her questions in a positive manner and never attempted to turn Jessica against her mother. "Maybe one day," Jessica once told him, "we will meet and I can ask her if she still loves me?" Jacob did not respond to her question. He did not know if his self-absorbed ex-wife would ever meet with their daughter again.

Brenda never did contact Jessica, but had the audacity to call Jacob the day before the funeral, from somewhere in Europe, to tell him she would not be attending. She said she would be a hypocrite coming to Jessica's funeral when she never attempted to be with her before her death. Without responding to her comments, Jacob slammed the phone against the wall with enough force to shatter the receiver into pieces. He was sure Brenda understood his reply.

Later that night, regaining his composure, he realized her decision not to attend might have been the best decision she ever made. Her presence would be of no value to Jessica, nor console anyone else.

For the next several months, Jacob received psychiatric therapy to help manage the traumatic aftermath of the tragedy. As the result of a few fine doctors and the encouragement and support of family and friends, he learned to cope with Jessica's death—not to accept or understand it, simply to cope.

After many distressing outbursts, the doctors helped him see that the accident was not his fault, nor Jessica's, and there was nothing more he could have done. Jacob was thankful for all they accomplished, but it would be a long time before he accepted that he could not have done more to save his child.

The doctors also helped him to suppress his hatred toward the seventeen-year-old driver who took Jessica's life. It was a stupid accident, by a teenage girl who said she did not see the stop sign, or Jessica. She hysterically acknowledged to police that she was talking to her girl friend on her cell phone; the topic: her boyfriend's new hairstyle.

Jacob's heart was seized with agony, when he was told at the hospital of the girl's explanation. "Jessica died," he said in disbelief, "because the driver could not wait to talk about her boyfriend's hair? Hair! A son-of-a-bitch hair style!" he yelled forcefully.

Lowering his voice, he said to the nurse, "Jessica has beautiful brown hair that flows to the middle of her back. I grab it when we play touch football, she screams at me to let it go, and then she falls to the ground laughing." He was telling the story as if Jessica were still alive. He stopped talking, fell back into the emergency room chair, and wept. Jacob had never been a vengeful man, but he felt satisfied to know that, like him, the driver would be haunted by the memories of Jessica's death forever.

The doctors, however, were not able to help him answer the enduring questions regarding God's role in Jessica's death. After all, Jacob thought, he had been raising Jessica as a Catholic, so why did God allow this atrocity to happen to an innocent child?

Why did God and Christianity abandoned them, he often asked himself. Would God have saved her if she followed the doctrine of Judaism or Islam, and not Christianity? After all, they worshipped the same God of Abraham, and maybe Christianity was not the way God wanted them to go?

In his heart, Jacob deeply wanted to believe in God, but through the conflicting messages of religion, he did not know what God wanted from him, or where to find God to ask Him. He remembered looking for God long before Jessica's birth, as a nineteen-year-old Marine hardened by warfare in the jungles of Vietnam. He sought answers from clerics as to why a loving God closed His eyes to the atrocities of war.

On the battlefield and his life in general, he asked himself and others, how does God decide who lives, is violently killed, endures anguish, mutilation, or dies alone in agony, pleading to God to help them. How can a loving God also be one of immense fury, condoning brutalities, yet expect our love in return?

No matter how often he searched for answers, the response from religious leaders consistently fell between "Because it is written," or "God works in mysterious ways, my son." Neither response satisfied Jacob then or after Jessica's death. He refused, however, to stop searching for answers.

He recalled meeting with his parish priest to discuss Jessica's violent fate. Although Father Acola was sincere, the response was the same Jacob had heard too often.

"Jacob, the answers you seek from God are within the scriptures of the New Testament, which I would be pleased to illuminate for you. As for the questions I cannot explain, you must remain strong in your faith and know that God often works in ways we do not comprehend. Jacob, you must continue to love Jesus Christ, as your family has done for generations. It is what Jesus wants you to do."

My family and religion, Jacob thought ruefully, as a slight smile that he hoped Father Acola would not misinterpret as a lack of attention, crossed his face.

He recalled his father answering his inquisitive questions with, "If God wanted you to know the answer, the priests at school would have taught you." A question he remembered asking one night over dinner when he was thirteen - was, "Dad or

Mom, how do we know the Bible is accurate and tells us the truth about how God wants us to live?"

His father's face grew so red that it seemed to blot out all other colors in the room, and his mother sat frozen with her forkful of food in mid-air. It was the longest period of silence Jacob had ever endured, at least an hour it seemed. But, after what could only have been a few seconds, his father responded sharply, "Jacob, this is not the first time we have told you it is sacrilegious to question your faith, or the writings of the Bible. At some point you have to believe, as your mom and I do. Accept your faith in Jesus Christ, son. Now!"

When his father finished, Jacob excused himself from the table and went upstairs to his room mumbling to himself, another night of unanswered questions, and no dinner.

Jacob responded to the good priest with kindness in his voice, "thank you, Father, but the scriptures do not remedy the pain in my heart, and in many respects, they have introduced more questions."

"Such as?" Father asked.

"For instance," Jacob replied. "If God is the one God of Judaism, Christianity and Islam, whose side is he on, and which scriptures and doctrines must I follow? I understand Christianity is the path you have chosen, and the one I have followed, yet, it did not save Jessica."

"Father," Jacob continued without giving the priest an opportunity to respond, "I simply am not sure anymore, and it is imperative now that I determine whether God is a Jew, Christian, Muslim, somewhere in-between, or none of the above. Then, I will know the ideology that will assure I find God. When I find

God, He will confirm there is a Heaven, resolve the contradictions of scriptures, and assure me that Jessica is safe with Him. Afterward, when it is my turn to depart this life I will know I am on the right road to join her. I promised her we would be together always, and I will not disappoint her again."

Father Acola tried again to respond, but Jacob cut him off once more, explaining that he had a meeting to rush to. Jacob was not emotionally prepared to engage in a discussion regarding the validity of the scriptures. His questioning of the accuracy of the scriptures was another reason he needed to find God. He was confused as to which of the thousands of scriptures were correct, why God gave instructions to only one person at a time, and why they were handed down in parables, thereby giving mankind the ability to devise a multitude of contradicting interpretations.

No, Jacob silently confirmed, he did not want to begin a discussion on scriptures. As he looked at the priest's weary expression, he sensed that he was in no hurry to discuss them either.

As Jacob was leaving, Father Acola said, "Travel safely. And may your heart find the answers you are seeking; Peace be with you, my son."

"And also with you," Jacob replied instinctively, as he was taught to do as a Catholic.

Jacob wondered if he would find God amid the diversity and contradictions of religion, or would he find that God exists only within the minds of people? Unlike his earlier attempts to find God, he was determined not to yield to doubt or complacency on this journey. Jessica had been his salvation in an otherwise humdrum life, yet he failed to protect her. He had to be sure now if she was at peace, and only God can provide the answer.

"Only God can provide the answer", he chuckled, as he repeated the statement. Yet, what if God decides not to enlighten him? After all, what would make Jacob A. Hinsen so special that God will meet him in secret to answer the questions men have been asking since the dawn of time?

Jacob paused as he considered his dilemma. He knew prior to Jessica's death that questions such as this would have provided an excellent excuse for him to avoid finishing his journey, but not this time, he told himself. If God would not enlighten him personally, at least he should be able to confirm the road of religion God wants him to pursue. There was no turning back, he concluded. Never!

Jacob decided to begin his journey on the roads of three of the world's great religions: Judaism, Christianity and Islam. He knew this decision was based on his familiarity with Christianity, and that in his heart he wanted to believe the God he was taught to worship was indeed dwelling in one of the three religions descended from Abraham.

PROMISES

Jacob sat alone in his disheveled office on an old sofa cloaked with his departed dogs' hair, stuffing research papers into his already-overburdened backpack. It was six months, almost to the day, since his daughter lost her life in the senseless accident. At fifty-eight, he was still a nice-looking man of average height and build, but above average intelligence. He possessed more than the intellect measured by standard IQ tests; he had seized upon the knowledge a person acquires though decades of rising above the challenges life randomly places before us all. No challenge, however, was greater than the one on which he was about to embark.

Unlike his earlier journeys, this time he began by charting the course he would travel, and cramming well thought-out essentials into his backpack. Obviously, he would need water and food, enough at least to keep him satisfied between destinations. Indispensable, too, were his documents: a condensed Bible, Internet research, synopses of various religious wars, and a collection of diverse commentaries on God's word by prominent religious leaders.

In the past he's been passionate, but not committed. Before, when the journey became difficult he found it easiest to surrender to the spiritual doctrine he knew best, but doing so only soothed his heart's petition for answers temporarily. This time he knew he had to be more than passionate; he must be conclusive.

Before he left he walked through his house to make certain everything was secure and in order, he had no idea how long he would be away. As he planned, his last stop was Jessica's room, but when he entered, an intense sorrow overwhelmed him. Perhaps, he thought, it was the realization that he was leaving for the first time since her death, and would not visit her room again for an unknown period.

He overcame his sadness; however, as he forced himself to think of positive events he shared with Jessica. He recalled the time when she was around four years old, and woke him one morning by pulling out his dresser drawers, and using them as a ladder climbed to the top. She then jumped from the dresser top to his bed, and then on to his stomach.

He grimaced as he remembered the weight of her landing, but smiled as he recalled how she tossed her small arms around his neck, hugged him and said, "I love you daddy." He would give anything to hear her say those four words again.

He blew Jessica a kiss as he closed her bedroom door behind him. He knew she was not there, but sometimes it felt good to pretend. After all, he thought, she is always in his heart, forever.

After six long days of traveling by air, train and hired local gypsy taxi drivers, Jacob reached the ancient Gateway of Abraham; the only entrance to The Kingdom of Religious Confusion. Once through its portal he would begin his journey on the war-torn roads of God's three religions.

From his position, he observed through the gate that one of the roads of religion was more opulent then the others. Another heralded the virtues of peace to all believers who endeavored to reach God. The third road was narrower and older, yet affirmed itself as the true road chosen by God.

Beyond the Gateway, he saw that while the roads of religion began near to each other, they soon alienated in vastly different directions extending far into the Kingdom of Religious Confusion, where he hoped to find God.

Breaking from his thoughts, Jacob stepped through the Gateway and selected the largest and most opulent road to travel. It was not the oldest road of religion, but it was the road most familiar to him. He remained steadfast, took a deep breath of faith, and stepped onto the glistening Road of Christianity.

THE ROAD OF CHRISTIANITY

The beauty of Christianity's pageantry and the allegiance of over two billion parishioners who proclaim it as their faith overwhelmed Jacob as he stepped onto the Road of Christianity. Within a few steps, however, the road divided before him again into two wide paths. One summoned him toward the path of Roman Catholics, the other to the path of the Protestants.

He could see indicators of wealth and power along both paths, but could also tell that they were not in every place. As with other religions, Jacob thought, Christianity features both the grandeur and wealth of a few and the poverty of many. He reminded himself to keep an open mind. He sought the truth, and so he needed to be patient and not prejudge how he thought things should be.

After all, he told himself, when I find God I will also find the reason why some people are rich and others poor and subject to strict religious and social boundaries. Jacob smirked as he thought how ridiculous this sounded, and hoped a loving God would agree.

Both paths were lined with majestic cathedrals where ceremonial rituals seized custody of believers' minds and souls. Rituals so captivating that they stimulate faith in Jesus Christ across all human senses. Beyond the cathedrals he noticed extravagant palaces constructed for esteemed Christian leaders. One palace Jacob he was familiar with was the Vatican. There, the Roman Catholic Pope resides, along with priceless treasures of ancient Christian art, architecture and literature. Jacob wondered if the opulence and rituals of Christianity was the way Jesus Christ wanted things to be.

Christian symbols were in abundance. Some were large, many small, and a multitude of tattered, hand-painted items were affixed indiscriminately to trees and buildings lining the road. The symbols beckoned seekers of God to chose from the independent paths of Roman Catholicism, Orthodox and other Eastern beliefs, Pentecostals, Baptists, Methodists, Anglicans, Lutherans, Jehovah's Witness, Mennonite, Christian Disciples of Christ, Amish, Episcopal, Mormon, Presbyterian, Seventh-Day Adventist, Quakers, Apostolic, and more.

He was exhausted trying to differentiate between them all. Although each symbol pointed toward a unique denominational path, they shared a common theme: "Follow this path, for it is the way to our Lord, Jesus Christ, and your salvation."

Jacob was already aware of these symbols and the great division in the Road of Christianity. It was at this point where he had previously quit looking for God on several occasions. The numerous paths to God overwhelmed him, and he could not tell which path God wanted him to travel.

He thought it would be easiest to select any one of them, and pray God understood his dilemma. However, this journey was different, he whispered to himself, this time he would not retreat from the challenge.

Determined to succeed, Jacob decided to seek out his old friend on the Path of Roman Catholicism.

Jacob knew that, with over a billion parishioners

following the path of Roman Catholicism, it was the single largest tradition in Christianity. He stood in awe as he observed parishioners moving in and out of religious gathering places. They reminded him of bees hovering outside hives, each with a specific purpose in support of the hive and queen bee.

In addition to parishioners, there were numerous cardinals, bishops and priests who governed their flocks of liturgical educators, other clergy, and laypeople.

"Father! Father Doyle!" Jacob yelled, as his focus turned to the priest walking into the rectory at St. Andrew's Church, "May we talk?"

After a long look, Father Doyle recognized Jacob and replied, "Absolutely Jacob, absolutely!" Jacob crossed the busy street and walked briskly up the steps to meet the priest. They reached out and embraced each other, as old friends do, without pretense.

"Where the hell have you been for the past thirty years, or how ever long it's been?" Father Alfred Doyle asked with great interest and enthusiasm.

Jacob responded with a broad smile, equally excited, and told him that it had, indeed, been more thirty years since they'd last seen each other. Over the next few hours, Jacob filled Father Doyle in on his life's events. Father asked him so many questions that he felt as though he'd been through a marathon confession after they'd finished talking. He was sure the priest would ask him to recite 2000 Hail Marys' for his sins, but Father Doyle seemed satisfied with knowing he was okay.

It was hard to believe, Jacob thought, but the last time they had talked for such a long time was when Jacob returned home from Vietnam and the carnage of war. A time in his life when he was engulfed in conflicting emotions as to who was right or wrong, bewildered as to why a loving God allowed gruesome atrocities to occur, and doubtful whether his assignments during combat were sanctified by God. He was also haunted by the guilt he harbored for returning home, while so many of his friends did not.

Jacob smiled as he recalled the many conversations they'd shared and how thankful he was to Father Alfred for listening to his anguish, as a friend. Father comforted him by speaking of the love of God, but did not pretend to know why God allowed terrible things to happen. Jacob respected his truthfulness and loved the priest as his dearest friend. To Jacob, Father Doyle demonstrated the love of God and never emphasized the punishments of God's wrath. Jacob often wondered if Father Doyle shared some of his doubts, but he respected him too much to ask.

Father Doyle was supportive when he heard about Jacob's divorce, and nothing saddened him more than Jessica's death. He wished he had the chance to be part of Jessica's life, and for several minutes, he prayed silently for her and Jacob. When he finished, he placed his hand on Jacob's shoulder and said, "I am sorry for your loss my son, and if I had known of the tragedy I would have come to you as a friend. If ever you need me, I am here for you. And, Jacob, know God is always with you."

Jacob saw the sadness in his mentor's eyes, and with a heartfelt smile gently replied, "There is no doubt in my mind, Father. I often thought of calling you, but –" Jacob stopped. He knew whatever he was about to say was no more than an excuse for not calling. How, he wondered, had he let the decades go by without contacting his friend? Jacob was saddened by the sudden recognition of his disrespect.

"Thank you, Father," Jacob said, as tears filled his eyes. He knew Father Doyle understood.

Jacob noticed that his friend had aged, but then so had he. He figured Father to be in his late eighties, yet he was still sharp, articulate and good-natured. Jacob remembered how the girls in his ninth grade class at St. Andrews School thought Father Doyle was gorgeous and wished he wasn't a priest so they could marry him when they got older. Of course, as soon as they said it they looked to heaven and asked God for forgiveness, just in case He was listening.

It became a joke for the boys to watch the girls from across the courtyard as they spoke and then looked heavenward for forgiveness. Jacob smiled at this memory, one from his pre-war life, memories he conditioned himself to forget after the horrors of Vietnam and certainly since Jessica's death.

Jacob knew that for over a quarter of a century, Father Doyle had been a pillar of his community and active in the Christian education of his congregation. His focus had always been on the youth of the parish and the adults who struggle to understand the disciplines and controversy of the Catholic faith. "The Bible is not perfect," Father would tell his students, "nor is man. Yet we must build on a foundation of beliefs in order to be at peace with God."

In contrast to many Christian educators, he believed questioning the status quo was a positive thing, because it challenges the educator, and strengthens people's faith. To him this philosophy was a simple approach to teaching, since he passionately believed God would one day bring all the lost souls who ventured into the chaos of religious thought back to him and the Catholic Church.

Jacob recalled how very different this approach was from Sister Mary Elizabeth Russell's teaching. She told him when he was an impressionable young boy of nine that if he did not stop asking questions about his religion, he would go straight to Hell. She had certainly scared the hell out him, he thought.

It was Father Doyle's openness and willingness to discuss religious differences that made him popular. When Jacob first met him he was eight years old, and, throughout his adolescent years, Father's mentorship was indispensable in helping Jacob understand himself and the religious confusion buried in his heart. At a young age, Jacob learned to love this devout messenger of God.

To bring Father back to the reason for his visit, Jacob summarized the purpose of his quest. As he watched Father Doyle's expression, he recognized his look. "Jacob," he imagined Father Doyle was thinking to himself, "haven't we discussed these same conflicts a hundred times before?" They probably had, more times than either man cared to remember.

The priest replied with enthusiasm, "Let the questioning begin!"

Jacob grabbed a handful of notes from his backpack, and eagerly began. "Father Alfred, why do Christians believe a person will only receive God's blessing by accepting Jesus

Christ?"   "The
straightforward answer", Father Doyle replied, "is because it is
written in the Gospels of Matthew, Luke, Mark and John, as well
as other holy scriptures of St. Paul, and the saints thereafter. It is
the essence of our belief as Christians."

"But why is Jesus the only way, and not one of the
ways?" Jacob asked, continuing, "What about the Jews and
Muslims who believe in the same God, but have chosen different
doctrines to reach Him?"

"I see I will need to be more specific in answering your
questions, Jacob," Father Doyle pleasantly replied. "I should
have remembered that simple answers never satisfied you, even
in your youth." Father Doyle removed his jacket and placed it
on the back of his chair. Jacob knew he was preparing for a
thoughtful discussion.

"Okay, let me begin again," Father Doyle said. "Our
Catholic faith, which has differences from other Christian faiths,
believes that Jesus is our Savior and the Son of God. This is
taught to us foremost in the scriptures of the New Testament and
the Epistles of our saints, a total of twenty-seven writings in all,
including several books from the Old Testament."

"Each of these scriptures was dictated, or influenced in
some way by God. Although there are some inconsistencies
caused by the translation of Hebrew to Greek, for instance,
together they are the result of what Catholic leaders have
discussed and agreed upon over centuries. Therefore, when I say
'Jesus Christ is the path to God,' it is because 'It is written. I

believe Saint John said it best," he continued from memory, "'Jesus saith unto him, I am the way, the truth, and the life, no man cometh unto the Father, but by me (John 14:6).'"

"Father," Jacob said, "you know I respect your teaching and faith, but if all three religions believe in the same God, why would God shun those who do not believe in Jesus Christ as the Son of God? After all, from Abraham to Muhammad many great prophets have taught the love and wisdom of God. Are those not valid teachings?"

"You have touched on the major difference of our religions, Jacob." Father Doyle replied, and continued, "You recall our belief is that Jesus Christ is more than a prophet, He is the Son of God. This is confirmed best in Matthew 3:16-17," which Father again quoted verbatim: "And when Jesus was baptized he went up immediately from the water, and behold, the heavens were opened and he saw the Spirit of God descending as a dove, and alighting on him; and lo, a voice from heaven, saying, 'This is my beloved Son, with whom I am well pleased."

"Nevertheless," Jacob responded, "the love, compassion and guidance taught through the alleged biblical teachings of Jesus are wonderful, but..." Before Jacob finished Father Doyle interrupted abruptly.

"What do you mean by the 'alleged' teachings of Jesus? The word of Jesus in our scriptures has been researched, debated and recorded by the greatest of scholars. There are no alleged teachings, Jacob. They are the accepted teachings of God, and canon of the Catholic Church."

Whoops! Jacob thought. He had hit a hot spot with the good Father. He sensed the priest was telling him that we need to believe, and that he chose to believe in the scriptures of the

Catholic Church. Jacob was not sure if he emphasized his response because he had no desire to debate the authenticity or accuracy of scripture.

Nevertheless, Jacob knew discussing the scriptures was essential to finding God. After all, it is the varying interpretations of scriptures, which have created the disparate paths of religions. If he can find the true scriptures, written by God without Man's intervention, then he will have the confirmation he needed.

"Father Alfred," Jacob continued, "you have chosen to believe in the Catholic Word of God, as recorded in the New Testament. If you don't mind, I would like to pursue this topic in more detail." Father Doyle gave one of those, 'Oh, what the Hell' smiles, and said, "Bring it on!"

Jacob continued, "Why were the scriptures written in a manner which allowed them to be subject to a wide range of interpretations? Even today, radical groups like the Klu Klux Klan can locate passages in the New Testament to justify their hate and racial discrimination."

"Scriptures," he continued, "are similar to tax laws. Instead of being easy to understand, they require lawyers and accountants to decipher the hidden code and manipulate, within reason, the outcomes. Therefore, wouldn't disagreement within Christianity be resolved if every Christian was only taught and adhered to the two greatest commandments?"

"You have outdone yourself with the simplicity of your suggestion," Father Doyle said to Jacob with a smile. "First, let me clarify the 'two greatest commandments' you refer to." As Jacob searched through his notes for the answer, Father Doyle recited both aloud:

"The first," he said, "is Matthew 22:37 to 38, where 'Jesus said unto him, Thou shalt love the Lord thy God with all thy heart, and with all thy soul, and with all thy mind..." The second, of course, begins in Matthew 22:39, 'Thou shalt love thy neighbor as thyself... On these two commandments hang all the law and the prophets."

"Yes, those are the two," Jacob responded. Before Father Doyle could continue, Jacob asked, "If Christianity taught and lived by only these two commandments, wouldn't there be fewer schisms between religious ideologies, fewer wars, and no debates regarding who God loves best? Do you know what I mean, Father?" Jacob's impatience sounded in his voice.

"I do know what you mean," Father replied. "And, I share your frustration, but I believe it will be a long time before mankind will reach the level of religious simplicity you are looking for. If God gave Man only those two Commandments, I am sure within a short period of time humankind would be debating the definition of 'love,' and if the love you give God is the same love you give your neighbor. Nevertheless Jacob, it is a wonderful thought."

Then Father Doyle said, "The majority of counseling I do is to help people learn to love themselves through Jesus Christ. Until they accept and love Jesus, they will never be able to love themselves, or their neighbors. You see, Jacob, as simple as your solution appears, people have to learn how to love. Through the teachings of Jesus Christ, this is done."

Jacob understood the point Father was making, but he had

serious reservations with the implementation of his philosophy. Jacob was going to ask Father why, if all Christians are taught to love and live peacefully through Jesus Christ, is there and abundance of hatred, wars, and butchery by Christians all done in Jesus' name? But he decided to hold his question for a later time, and brought the conversation back to the scriptures.

"Is it possible," Jacob pressed, that the scriptures were modified over the centuries by social, military or political chaos? After all, a religion's faith is based on its leaders' interpretation of scripture and ancient manuscripts. For example, Judaism, Christianity and Islam share some of the same scriptures, yet disagree on the interpretation and intent of essential passages. Similar disagreements occur within Christianity, where the Roman Catholic interpretation is different from the Lutherans,' which is different from the Methodists,' who differ from the Orthodox, et cetera."

"That said, Father, my question is this: since there remains great controversy within Christianity regarding the accuracy of scriptures, why do you even now believe the Catholic interpretation is correct? What proof is there any scriptures touched by man are accurate?"

Jacob sensed irritation in Father Doyle's face when he asked the question; as if it was one he had been asked too many times. He did not intend to put Father Doyle on the defensive, but he needed to understand what proof was strong enough to keep a great man such as him believing that Catholicism was the only way to find God.

"Faith, my dear friend," Father Doyle replied firmly. "Faith, not proof, is what binds me to Catholicism and Jesus Christ."

"No!" Jacob thought to himself. That was not what he wanted to hear. Father Alfred had to know more. He could not have spent decades believing in words that told of things he has neither seen, nor touched. Before he could ask another question, Father Doyle continued as if he'd read Jacob's mind.

"You and I do not have the ability or knowledge to confirm scriptures or other events which happened centuries ago. Nevertheless, there have been constructive debates, scientific confirmation, and yes, some speculation regarding the validity of our Bible's texts, both the Old and New Testaments."

Father Doyle continued and Jacob did not intend to interrupt him. "When a person has researched their questions, debated the answers and reached an individual decision, they have two options: remain steadfast about what they believe is true, even if empirical proof is not available, or they continue to search for alternative pathways to God, should they even exist. I have satisfied myself Jacob that Jesus Christ is the way; therefore I believe what is written."

Father Doyle leaned over and looked deep into Jacob's eyes, saying, "At some time, Jacob, in your short life on Earth you will have to acknowledge absolute belief in a direction. If not, you will find yourself searching and never finding peace."

Jacob thought this might be okay if an individual accepted unconditionally what had been written in scripture, but didn't it also mean they had not necessarily found God? He wondered if he didn't settle on a specific ideology and continued to search for God if his life would really be devoid of peace. What if finding

God is a journey toward spiritual growth through the teachings of many philosophies, not restricted to a single interpretation of God's Word?

What if! What if! What if! Jacob thought to himself as he turned his attention back to what the good Father was saying.

"Even an atheist," Father Doyle continued, "acknowledges absolute belief in a theory. Even though they have cracks in their beliefs, such as not being able to explain the origin of the tiny speck of energy said to have exploded to create our universe. All the same, they are as adamant that they are correct as any religion's followers."

"Nice parallel," Jacob replied. "Father, have you no concern with the scriptures as they are written and interpreted?"

"I don't, Jacob yet it appears that you do. So, let's talk about your dilemma, because it is important to you."

"Father", Jacob said softly; "I have so many questions that I'm not sure where to begin."

Before Jacob could continue, he was interrupted by three sharp knocks on the rectory door. Thump! Thump! Thump! They repeated loudly. Each knock resonated through the rectory hall with an eerie cadence that reminded Jacob of the sounds from an old haunted house movie.

Father Doyle did not seem surprised as he rose from his chair and walked to the door. Interruptions were common. As he opened it, he blocked Jacob's view of the figure standing in the doorway. Jacob could not hear what was said, but he gasped as he recognized the portly man standing before him.

Bathed in the sunlight radiating through the rectory door was Cardinal Abbott Leopold, Jacob's worst nightmare.

As the two holy men walked toward him he rose from his chair and extended his hand to greet his former high school principal. Jacob's thoughts raced back to the day he was called to His Eminence's office for swearing on the playground. He sat fearfully on a hard wooden chair as Father Leopold, as he was known then, stared at him for what seemed like hours.

After what was only a few minutes, Father Leopold rose from his chair, maintaining eye contact all the while, and cracked a ruler so hard across the top of his desk that Jacob thought he might have wet his pants. The giant man bellowed, "Don't ever let me see you back in my office again, or you will think Satan is an evangelist! Is that clear?"

"Yes, your Highness!" Jacob shouted in terror, calling the priest by the wrong title.

"Now, get out!" Father Leopold yelled. The next thing Jacob remembered was sitting at his classroom desk, uncertain of how he got there. To this day, he wondered if it happened by some "priestly magic," or God. After so many years, Jacob felt confident the aged priest did not remember the event. During introductions, he was relieved to find that the Cardinal did not seem to remember him.

Given their vastly different personalities, Jacob was surprised to learn that the semi-retired cardinal was Father Doyle's mentor and friend, and often visited him unannounced.

Jacob caught the gleam in Father Doyle's eyes as he led

the cardinal to a chair in the corner of the room, one evidently reserved for him alone. The patience he showed while helping the elderly man to his chair revealed the tremendous respect and love he had for him.

In contrast with Father Doyle, Cardinal Leopold was a strict teacher of the Catholic faith, a member of the "Old Guard," Jacob thought to himself. He spoke of God's love, but ruled his congregation by advocating God's wrath.

Meeting the cardinal for the first time after many years brought on a sense of uneasiness in Jacob's stomach. He did not want to be that young boy again, sitting across from the principal's desk, alone and defenseless, in the presence of religious authority. He had to be stronger, and he would be, he told himself.

Jacob heard Father Doyle as he brought the cardinal up to speed on their conversation, but did not hear mention of Jessica or other names from his past. Jacob appreciated Father Doyle's discretion.

"Your Eminence," Jacob began, feeling a little intimidated but glad to have another cleric's response to his questions. "Thank you for agreeing to discuss my questions. Father Doyle and I have been in conversation for several hours, but both of us feel your perspective is of great value." Cardinal Leopold looked at him and smiled as Jacob felt a small twinge of his old fear.

"The question I have pertains to the accuracy of the Holy Scriptures," Jacob said. But before he was able to continue, Cardinal Leopold raised his right hand in a gesture to stop the question, as if to indicate that he had heard these uncertainties thousands of times and was not interested in hearing them again.

In a voice that was firm, yet far from the thunderous voice he remembered from the youth, Cardinal Leopold spoke.

"My son, your confusion is not unique. Each of us has been on the same journey at some point in our lives. It is important that you understand you are neither alone, nor the first. Please, go ahead and share with us your concerns, confusion and doubts. I am sure Father Doyle and I will be able to provide you with some answers. If that is agreeable to you, please proceed."

Well, Jacob thought, there goes my fear of Cardinal Leopold. He had either softened over the course of his eighty-nine years, or become bored answering the same questions, over and over again. Whatever! it was time to take advantage of the moment.

"Thank you your Eminence, and Father Doyle," Jacob replied. "I'm sure this is not new news to you, but the many interpretations of religious scriptures has created great schisms between religions and peoples of the world, not only between Judaism, Christianity, and Islam, but within Christianity itself. Protestants against Catholics for instance."

Both men nodded their heads to indicate they understood where the questioning was headed.

"Please don't get me wrong, I'm not questioning whether Jesus existed, or exists. But, given the agreement within the Church that men played a pivotal role in the development of Christian scriptures, I am confused why you believe Jesus Christ, is the only way to salvation and the Kingdom of God."

Father Doyle was going to answer, but Cardinal Leopold

stopped him, indicating he wanted to respond. The elder man said, "Please give a few examples of the inconsistencies and man's intervention that you are referring to."

"By some accounts," Jacob said, "the first scriptures were not written down until around 70 or 150 AD, many years after Jesus' resurrection. Therefore, much of what was written was passed down orally, as people told others, who told others, et cetera. Even if we agree that the tellers of the tales, for lack of a better name, were good people of God with the best of intentions to quote the stories verbatim, there had to be misinterpretations from language translations, missing or partial passages, or even a manipulation of stories to support a church or secular leader's demands."

Cardinal Leopold nodded for him to go on, but Jacob was hesitant, not knowing how far he should push for answers. He did not want the conversation to turn into a defensive debate, after all, he was questioning the foundation of Christianity. Yet if he avoided asking the hard questions, he would never find his answers. He continued.

"Many of the writers of the New Testament are not known. In the cases of Luke, Matthew and Paul, none of them met, walked with, or experienced the teachings of Christ first hand. As great a Christian as Saint Paul was through his teachings to the Gentiles; he had considerable disputes with Peter and the original Apostles over the messages he was teaching."

"And, Luke, or maybe it was Mark, who are identified as authors of the gospels, and Matthew were heavily influenced by

Paul, not Jesus himself. I apologize," Jacob added, "if I have the saints mixed up. Anyhow, the concept is the same."

Jacob paused and looked at both men. He thought for sure the cardinal would stop him to a least question the origin of the information he was quoting, but neither man made any move to stop him. He assumed it was because they have heard the same narratives so many times that they simply listen until the speaker is done to answer. If that was the case, he appreciated their patience and continued.

"When differences in doctrine threatened to split the Christian Church around 325, at the First Ecumenical Council of Bishops in Nicaea, the scriptures as we know them today were selected by a group of clergymen. They poured over thousands of manuscripts and fifty different versions of the Bible. But, only 300 of the 1800 bishops in the Roman Empire attended to debate and vote on which scriptures should be included.

To further complicate matters, the Church was under great pressure from the Roman Emperor, Constantine, to compile a single Christian canon. But how did the bishops and scholars know which scriptures to dispose of, and those to include? "

"Shall I continue?" Jacob asked.

"Yes," Father Doyle replied. Sensing Jacob had the impression they were bored with his information. Father Doyle said, "I am sure you understand, Jacob, we have heard these arguments many times. Nevertheless, we are impressed with the research you have gathered. Please continue."

Jacob smiled at his friend, but was not sure His Eminence shared the opinion. Cardinal Leopold stared at him and only gave an occasional nod of his head. Jacob reminded himself that he was no longer a chastened, intimidated little boy.

"Subsequent councils continued to settle open issues, but not with the full agreement of the Christian elders. Critical differences in opinion about the relationship of the Trinity, God in three persons, the Father, Son and Holy Sprit, arose, as did debates regarding the divine and human nature of Jesus. The Roman and Eastern churches split at this time over the issue.

In 447, at the Synod of Toledo, in Spain, the Filoque Clause changed the Nicene Creed to add, 'of the Son' to show that the Holy Spirit came from both God the Father, and the Son, Jesus Christ. This, I believe, is still a point of disagreement between Roman and Orthodox Christian churches."

Jacob had more examples and plenty of notes to keep going, but he was weary of reciting known events in Christianity to an audience more knowledgeable than he was. He also did not want to appear to have a personal feud with Christianity. He was only looking for his long-sought answers.

"Sirs," Jacob said, "My question once more is with the uncertainties in the evolution, sorry maybe that is the wrong word to use, of scriptures: why does the Catholic Church believe there is no other way to God except through Jesus Christ?"

The Cardinal responded to him again, and was both succinct and philosophical. "Your questions are similar to those that many people have struggled with since the beginning of Christianity, or any religion for that matter. We have all questioned the mystery of our faith."

"Even you and Cardinal?" Jacob asked with surprise.

"Yes, even me," the Cardinal continued. "We have found that believers reach an understanding of faith at different times in their lives, and under a variety of circumstances."

As he spoke, Jacob realized that he was not intimidated by the senior cleric any longer. He wondered if it was because he had outgrown the fear of God taught to him as a young boy in Catholic school. Or, was it because he has realized over the years that there never was a reason to fear a loving God? He had no intention of pondering the reason at that time, he needed to listen to the Cardinal.

"Your concerns appear to pertain to the authenticity and accuracy of our scriptures. Realizing of course they are two different areas of discussion, for simplicity I will answer your concerns as if authenticity and accuracy are one concern. We always have the option to revisit a specific answer. You also must understand that you have limited us to providing you only our personal knowledge and beliefs, since showing you the answers in Bible Scripture would not satisfy your doubts. OK?"

"Yes, Your Eminence." Jacob replied. The Cardinal then moved from his chair to sit across the table from Jacob, as Jacob continued speaking. "I am sure you understand my uncertainty as it pertains to religious scriptures in general. They have been written and modified by men, and create the foundation for the control of people in God's name. Wars, genocide and other atrocities are referenced in scripture with God's blessing," Jacob finished, his frustration coming through in his voice.

Cardinal Leopold patted him on the shoulder and handed him several documents he had removed from Father Doyle's bookshelf. "I would like ask you to read a few passages to us from our Catholic Catechism. You may have read them long ago, but I am not sure if you remember them."

"Our catechism," Cardinal Leopold continued, "is the day-to-day guidebook bishops, priests and educators use to teach Catholic doctrine. In Article 2, under 'The Transmission of Divine Revelation,' it describes how the Catholic Church considers scriptures to be one way of interpreting God's word. The other is through the tradition of the Catholic Church. By tradition, I mean that, when a scripture is unclear or inconsistent, the religious community, in our case the Pope and the Roman Catholic Church's senior clergy, interpret them to establish clarity."

"But if that's the case," Jacob interjected, "Does that mean that, over the centuries, men have granted themselves the authority to change scripture?"

"We'll get to that soon enough," Leopold replied.

The cardinal handed Jacob a copy of the Catechism and asked him to read paragraphs 80 through 82. Jacob read each passage as requested: "Section 80, Sacred Tradition and Sacred Scripture, are bound closely together, and communicate one with the other. For both of them, flowing out from the same divine well-spring, come together in some fashion to form one thing, and move towards the same goal. Each of them makes present and fruitful in the Church the mystery of Christ, who promised to remain with his own always, to the close of the age."

"Continue please," the Cardinal asked.

"Section 81: 'the Sacred Scripture is the speech of God as it is put down in writing under the breath of the Holy Spirit. And

[Holy] Tradition transmits in its entirety the Word of God, which has been entrusted to the apostles by Christ the Lord and the Holy Spirit. It transmits it to the successors of the apostles so that, enlightened by the Spirit of truth, they can faithfully preserve, expound and spread it abroad by their preaching.'

"And Section 82 states that as a result 'the Church, to whom the transmission and interpretation of Revelation is entrusted, does not derive her certainty about all revealed truths from the Holy Scriptures alone. Both Scripture and Tradition must be accepted and honored with equal sentiments of devotion and reverence.'"

"Therefore," Cardinal Leopold exclaimed, "we determine our doctrine through the scriptures, which we accept have some imprecision, combined with the traditions of the Roman Catholic Church. Since we believe the Catholic Church, meaning the teachings and faith, to be infallible, so are the modified scriptures."

Jacob understood when it came to the acceptance of infallibility, a person either believed it to be true, or didn't. The priest and the cardinal believed it, but Jacob had deep reservations that a person or group of people could be infallible. Besides, he rationalized, if religious leaders are infallible, it leaves little need for God.

Nevertheless, Jacob concluded that debating their belief against his speculation would be of no value to the conversation. He knew none of them had met directly with God, so the discussion would be based on individual faith or opinions.

This was the same challenge Jacob wrestled with when it came to religion in general. Without tangible proof from God, religions and devout followers adamantly argue that their ideologies are the final commandments provided by God. Jacob realized his mind was wandering to questions only God could answer. He refocused his attention on the conversation in time to hear Leopold emphasize,

"...As important is what Jesus told us after His resurrection and redemption. He would send the Apostles the Spirit of Truth, better known as the Holy Spirit. It is through the Holy Spirit the Apostles, saints, popes and other church leaders, continue to learn the truth and the way."

Father Doyle added, "It's because of the teachings of the Holy Spirit that it was not necessary for some of the first Church leaders to have been with Jesus themselves to receive His message. To answer one of your earlier questions, we don't worry about St. Paul, St. Matthew, and others being able to preach the glory and wisdom of Jesus Christ without having walked by His side."

Cardinal Leopold waited for him to finish and added, "And, you're right, Jacob, for the first 300 years Christianity was in search of itself, while expanding at a pace faster than anyone imagined. This was good news, but it also allowed the development of many variations of individual teachings that were not the true teachings of Jesus. Many were closer to the philosophies of the Roman government, and some developed for personal reasons. All of this took place within an environment of religious fervor. It was a time when multiple gods were still worshiped, and religious prosecution was the norm."

As he finished, they noticed Cardinal Leopold seemed exhausted. Father Doyle asked him if he'd like to call it a night, and the older man nodded in agreement.

Before he left, the Cardinal stared deep into Jacob's eyes and, once again, Jacob felt like the scared little boy in the principal's office. After a long moment, the Cardinal said in a firm voice, "As for you young man, the things we have said may seem simplistic, but there will come a time in your life when you will understand that all things are not explained to us within the boundaries of Mankind's knowledge. Faith, even though you might call it 'blind faith,' allows us to live within Man's limited knowledge, until we have transcended in spirit to receive God's great wisdom."

Then, as an afterthought, he whispered to Jacob, "I almost wet my pants laughing as I watched you jump from your chair and run out of my office."

Jacob was at a loss for words. He remembered, the old cardinal remembered him!

Cardinal Leopold still smiling from seeing the shock on Jacob's face, said good night to both men, gave them God's Blessing through the sign of the cross, and let himself out the door.

Father Doyle poured a glass of wine for each of them. They sat in silence for a moment, each reflecting on the Cardinal's final message. Then in unison they toasted the man, and his legacy.

"He remembered me," Jacob said in a soft voice, so not to be heard. "He remembered me."

As they sipped their wine, Jacob sat back in his chair and

relaxed. Father Doyle recognized Jacob's expression and said, "You have more questions, don't you?"

"Yeah, are you up for it?"

"Sure."

"For the moment" Jacob said; "let's assume I agree with you that the scriptures are accurate." The priest smiled, and shook his head as if saying to himself, 'you still don't get it do you Jacob.' Jacob decided not to pause, and continued his question.

"If the scriptures are accurate, then why doesn't the Church follow them? It seems changes were made only to accommodate the Church or Emperors."

"I'm sure you have some examples in mind?"

"Yes." Jacob responded. "For instance, in the Ten Commandments, God instructed Moses not to worship any god but God and prohibited idolatry."

Father Doyle nodded.

Jacob continued, "Since Catholics teach the one way to God the Father is through the Son, Jesus Christ, isn't that placing another God, Jesus, before the God of Abraham? Also, are not the images and statues of Jesus on the Cross, the Virgin Mary, each of the saints, and even the painting of God on the ceiling of the Sistine Chapel, considered idolatry? Both seem to contradict what Moses said."

"You have an excellent talent for combining multiple questions into one. I'll take each of them one at a time." The priest replied.

"First, as Cardinal Leopold said, the scriptures and traditions of the Catholic Church determine our faith, as when the Council of Nicaea condemned the Arian teaching as heresy."

Jacob had never heard of the Arian teachings before and asked for an explanation.

"The Arian teaching argued that the Son, Jesus, was only a man, that He was neither equal to, nor co-eternal with God the Father. The other Christian groups of the time believed that God exists as three persons: Father, Son, and Holy Spirit, who are united as one. The Church leaders denounced the Arian teaching because we do not place Jesus before God because they are One."

Jacob was confused and agitated as he realized again that a small group of men had been able to make significant changes to the doctrine of the divinity of Jesus. "Do you mean," he asked, "that only those who participated at Nicaea decided on the essence of Jesus, and then condemned the Arian teaching?"

"Yes, though it wasn't as simple as that."

Jacob pressed the question. "But what about smaller Christian, Jewish and Muslim sects who believe there is one God of Abraham, the Father, and that the Trinity is incorrect, a heresy even?"

"That's a good question and, as Christians, we have reservations about the teachings of their religious doctrines. God will be the judge of who is right or wrong. I can only tell you what is written."

"As for idolatry, this question, too, was debated for several centuries before it was resolved at the Second Council of Nicaea . It was argued and agreed that representing Christ's human likeness in icons reinforces the doctrine of Jesus' manifestation as a man. It's not the same as the idol worship of the Golden Calf in the Old Testament, were the calf was treated as a god."

"Father, with all due respect, when people pray to a statue of a saint, or kiss a crucifix, isn't that the same as idol worship? In fact, I've heard some people bury a statue of St. Joseph face down in their backyard in order to sell their home."

"I don't know what some people do with their statues, but I'm sure they didn't hear about planting St. Joseph in the dirt from the pulpit. As for Jesus, I explained before, it's not the same at all. Jesus appeared first as man. He was not an image or a man-made symbol of a deity no one had seen. Jesus was visible and walked with men, and if cameras were around we'd have pictures of Him. We don't worship the icon of Jesus; we worship God, who is also Jesus."

Jacob was silent for a moment. He was still perplexed how men justified changes to the earlier commandments of God. Nevertheless, it was two in the morning, and evident that Father Doyle was ready to call it a night. But, he still had one question.

Jacob thought carefully about how to ask his last question. It was a hypothetical one, but one he hoped someday to have answered by God. He wanted to know whether God is a God of love, or a God of absolute rule with no tolerance for mankind's ignorance.

Finally, Jacob asked, "Let's say some archeologists discover new scriptures, and scholars of religion agree they prove Jesus Christ was a great prophet but not the Son of God. Then what?"

Father Doyle's reaction was immediate, and for the first time Jacob sensed irritation from him.

"Jacob, that is a hypothetical question, and one not in the realm of my personal belief. But, you know that if it happened, it would crush the foundation of our Christian faith."

"But," Jacob replied, "do you believe in your heart that after the love and devotion you have given to Jesus, the righteous way in which you've led your life, and the absolute love you've given others, that the God of Abraham would turn His back on you, even if you succumbed to human weaknesses? Is that really what a loving God would do?"

In a soft, tired voice the answer came, "Jacob, I have resolved these questions in my heart and have no doubt that Jesus Christ is God and the keeper of the path I will follow. God's Word has been given to us in scripture, and validated through the Catholic Church. Jesus Christ is the way we will enter heaven and receive God's blessing. There will always be questions, and some of them will never be answered to our human satisfaction. At some point in life, however, a person has to decide on their approach to God and embrace the authenticity of that belief."

"But Father, isn't that blind faith?"

"Call it what you will Jacob, I describe it just as faith. I'm not blind, nor am I blinded to the fact the Catholic Church hasn't progressed fast enough toward Christ. We are not God, Jacob. We are human beings, and therefore subject to failure. It's how we grow after we fail, that you must consider in your search for God.

"That's why I'm confident God will bring you back to me, and to the path of Roman Catholicism. We will continue to change as leaders, and transform our ideologies, as we grow in spirituality. For example, in 2000, Pope John Paul II said that, while there are grave deficiencies between the Catholic Church and other religions, a person who lives in accordance with Jesus' blessings, as described in the eight Beatitudes will enter the Kingdom of God."

"That, Jacob, was a milestone for the Catholic Church. It meant that other religions do not have to agree Jesus is God to enter Heaven, just follow His teachings."

Jacob found this last statement confusing. It maintained that the Catholic Church was still the way to God, but that non-Catholic souls were salvageable if they lived by Jesus' teachings. Jacob wasn't sure, nor did he ask if this meant there would be separate groups in Heaven for various categories of believers? Regardless, it was too late to press for the answer, and he was not sure the answer was even relevant at this point. He speculated if everyone, including Christians, lived by the peaceful teachings of Jesus Christ, the world would be a better place.

The men were tired, and, as if in silent agreement, both rose from their chairs to embrace in friendship.

After exchanging well wishes and optimism that their paths would cross again, they walked to the rectory door. Father Doyle asked Jacob to let him know what decision he made, and Jacob promised he would. As he turned to open the door Father Doyle placed his hand on Jacob's shoulder, made the sign of the cross and said, "In the name of the Father, and of the Son, and of the Holy Spirit, Amen. May peace be with you!"

"And also with you," Jacob replied as he walked down the steps looking toward the next path he would travel.

Exhausted, Jacob rented a room at an inexpensive roadside motel for the night. Before falling asleep he reviewed his notes and recorded his feelings in his journal. His mind was racing trying to recall each discussion, not just what was said, but also the manner in which Father Doyle and Cardinal Leopold responded verbally and physically. He took note of the same body and facial cues he learned to observe through years of arguing cases in court. He sensed when the men were reluctant to continue a line of questioning or so steadfast in their opinion there would be no room for compromise or further discussion.

His mood turned melancholy as he recognized many of his doubts and unanswered questions lingered regarding the accuracy of Christian scriptures as the only Word of God. He loved Father Doyle and respected his and the cardinal's devotion, but where was the proof that God wanted him to follow the Path of Roman Catholicism?

Proof! He thought to himself as if the word had never entered his mind before. Sure, it was proof, not theory he was searching for. Yet he never thought about what form the truth would come to him. Did he expect God to walk up to him and say, "Congratulations Jacob, you found me." Or contact him through an angel or burning bush? After all, God met with other men, why not him? Jacob knew the journey through the Kingdom of Religious Confusion would be difficult, but now he feared finding proof might be impossible.

Turning his attention back to his journey he knew to reach the Path of Protestants, he had to trek across a couple of side streets located on the Path of Roman Catholicism. He removed the map from his backpack to verify that the shortest route would be a left onto Born Again Street, followed by a right turn onto Fundamentalist Drive. He shoved the map back into his backpack and began the next part of his journey.

There didn't appear to be a vast difference between the Paths of Roman Catholicism and Protestants, yet there was enough divergence between the interpretation of the same scriptures to sponsor centuries of hatred and war between the ideologies. Jacob wondered which ideology had the "missing link" scripture that showed where Jesus taught that belligerence, mass murder, and religious rivalry were good deeds; he was sure neither group had one.

Nevertheless, to be sure of his assumptions he removed the small copy of the New Testament from his backpack and read the beatitudes again. As he knew, there were no directives from Jesus to hate or kill not even one's enemy. Jacob tore the page from the book, folded it and placed it in his shirt pocket for future reference. Even if he had doubts about the accuracy and authenticity of the scriptures, Jacob knew Christianity accepted them, even if its powerful leaders did not necessarily honor them.

Continuing again toward his destination Jacob was curious as to how many of the beatitudes he remembered from his years of Catholic education. Pulling the torn page from his pocket he was pleasantly surprised as he read the list aloud, and except for a few missing words he remembered most of them. He smiled when he realized he had forgotten how powerful these words were to him as a young boy. He read them one more time before putting them back in his pocket.

> Blessed are the poor in spirit, for theirs is the kingdom
> of heaven.
> Blessed are those who mourn, for they shall be
> comforted.
> Blessed are the meek, for they shall inherit the earth.
> Blessed are those who hunger and thirst for
> righteousness,
> for they shall be satisfied.
> Blessed are the merciful, for they shall obtain mercy.
> Blessed are the pure in heart, for they shall see God.
> Blessed are the peacemakers, for they shall be called
> sons of God.
> Blessed are those who are persecuted for
> righteousness' sake, for theirs is the kingdom of
> heaven.

What happened to following God's Word? Jacob wondered. He hoped God would tell him. He reached Born Again Street.

Born Again Street was swarming with Christians who had confessed their sins and received a personal revelation from Jesus Christ. Jacob thought it was great for those who were "saved," but the dilemma he had was that, once "born again," most people on the street wanted everyone else to accept the same zealous commitment to Jesus with no room for compromise. Take Ernie, for instance, the born-again Christian Jacob met during his travels.

"Hello, beautiful day isn't it?" Ernie asked with a warm, friendly smile.

"Absolutely," Jacob replied, reaching out to shake Ernie's hand. "How long have you lived on Born Again Street?"

"I moved to the neighborhood about two months ago, as soon as I was saved through the Lord Jesus Christ." Ernie told him, his smile still glowing.

Thinking he already knew how Ernie would answer, Jacob said, "Finding Jesus is wonderful, and I'm glad you've found your path to God. I'm on a quest of my own, and trying to locate the right path which will take me to God."

Ernie interrupted with genuine passion in his voice saying, "Your search is over my friend, and Jesus Christ is the way. Take it from a former sinner, I too have traveled the paths of religion and found the only path to God is when you accept Jesus Christ into your heart." Jacob thought this was what Ernie would say.

"That's wonderful," Jacob replied, "May I ask you another question?

"Certainly."

"Given there are hundreds, if not thousands, of interpretations of religious scriptures, which shape as many ideologies all proclaiming to be the true path to God, what if Jesus is not the only way to God?"

"What did you ask me?" Ernie asked appearing confused.

"Let me rephrase my question. What if you discover Jesus Christ is not the only way to God, or in fact is not God?"

"That is a stupid question! All other roads to God are flawed. Jesus is God, there is no way this is the wrong path." Ernie proceeded to explain that he has read the teachings of Jesus in scripture repeatedly. More importantly, since accepting Jesus his pain and burdens were gone, and he loved others now more than himself.

Jacob thanked Ernie for his time and turned to go. He heard Ernie yell, "Jesus loves you, Jacob!"

"And, he also loves you, Ernie!" Jacob yelled back.

Writing later in his journal, Jacob thought back on their meeting. He admired Ernie's commitment to his ideology, but at the same time saddened by his unyielding position that all other roads to God were false.

As he reached the intersection of Born Again Street and Fundamentalist Drive, Jacob noticed a group of people kneeling for mid-day worship services. Yet they all turned and watched him with suspicion. He felt a trace of apprehension as he returned their stares.

He read somewhere those living on Fundamentalist Drive fervently adhered to their interpretations of the scriptures, and don't accept others who do not share their ideology. This meant believing Jesus Christ is the Son of God, no questions asked. Otherwise, you are branded a heretic or infidel and subject to consequences, which they deem appropriate.

He did not want to stand out or interrupt the religious services in progress. His objective was to take Fundamentalist Drive for several blocks to reach the Path of Protestants. He decided there was no value discussing ideology with clerics whose position on God was absolute, and all other paths sacrilegious.

After a short distance, he could see the Path of Protestants not more than six or eight blocks away; he was glad to be leaving this area. He could never understand why most religions believe they are right and others wrong. Did a caring God really command the people he created to compose thousands of contradictory scriptures for their followers to recite while annihilating other who did not believe the same way? If that's the case, he thought, God must truly be setting us up to fulfill the prophecy of Armageddon.

Jacob's thoughts were interrupted when someone called to him, "Mr. Hinsen, do you have a moment?"

He froze; who on Fundamentalist Drive knew him, and why did they call him "Mr. Hinsen"? Jacob cautiously replied,

"Yes, who's there?"

"Dr. Allan T. Campbell," the voice replied, as a man emerged from the darkness of the alley onto the lighted path. He was tall and dark, but not handsome. Dr. Campbell extended his hand to Jacob, with a gracious smile as Jacob asked, "How do you know my name, have we met before?"

"No, we've never met, yet I know many things from my travels along the paths of religion. I guess you can say I represent the True Word of God."

"The True Word of God?" Jacob responded skeptically. "I'm not sure I understand?"

Campbell sneered at the question, as two other men approached and joined him. Neither man smiled nor spoke, and appeared to be waiting for instructions. Jacob assumed they were Campbell's bodyguards.

"You have chosen to travel quickly on the Path of Fundamentalists, yet you claim to be 'looking for God." Campbell asked.

"Yes," Jacob replied, trying to conceal his uneasiness. "I'm heading to the Path of Protestants."

"We know where you're headed, but why does a man doubting God travel upon our sanctified path? You aimlessly search for God, because you question your faith and the Holy Scriptures. You are a heretic, am I correct?" Campbell asked, his voice dripping with sarcasm.

Jacob tried to ignore the questions and made a move to pass the man standing in front of him, but Campbell and his men stood their ground blocking all directions. Jacob's nervousness escalated into fear.

"No, Dr. Campbell," Jacob managed to answer while gaining some control over his voice. "I'm not an infidel, heretic or any other name you choose to give to those who don't share your beliefs." Gaining more confidence, he continued, "I am a man confused by the many interpretations of God's Word as written in the Torah, New Testament and Quran. I don't know if God is on your side, or one of the other religions,' so I'm looking for God to ask Him."

Campbell was surprised by the firmness of Jacob's answer. However, his response was immediate and condescending. "You expect to speak to God if you find Him? If you must find Him that means you do not believe in Him. Your disbelief desecrates the sacred path of those who do not need empirical proof God exists. Your disbelief is blasphemous, Mr. Hinsen. Blasphemous!"

"I want to believe in God!" Jacob replied, his voice cracking, "That's why I'm searching until I find Him. I don't doubt God and I don't doubt your beliefs. Yet for now, at least, I do not share your steadfast faith. I am on this quest to find answers that may even lead me back to the same path you travel." Now it seemed the three men were at least listening. "God, Dr. Campbell, is not who I'm questioning, it's the inconsistencies between religions I'm trying to clarify."

Jacob thought he stated his case well, damn well! He waited for Campbell to respond.

One of the men handed Campbell some papers and

whispered into his ear. He took a few steps back and flipped through the documents before speaking again.

"Mr. Hinsen, we are committed to our faith and nothing you say will make us change those beliefs. Nor, do we accept the feeble rhetoric of others, like you, who trample upon our path for their convenience. This path is our faith, and you have ill-used it to shorten your travels to other pagan religions.

Jacob was frightened once more; he didn't want to be branded a pagan or heretic by these religious extremists. His left eye muscle began to twitch, the same way it had on the battlefields of Vietnam.

Without warning, Campbell's men grabbed hold of his arms and held him firmly as Campbell said, "Your punishment for the blasphemy of our faith will now be determined and swiftly executed."

"You have to be kidding," Jacob yelled. "This is the twenty-first century; you can't punish someone because they may have different beliefs than you!"

Jacob thought quickly, his plan was simple: to escape without killing unless he absolutely had to. He would knee the guy holding his left arm hard between his legs, at the same time pulling and then pushing the man on his right side into Campbell. The most he hoped for was to break free of them and run like hell to the Path of Protestants, to safety.

Jacob was about to tell the three men they were lunatics, but before he could, Campbell raised his right hand to silence him. Jacob complied.

Campbell spoke firmly, but not as arrogantly as before, "You say you look for God, and I tell you God is on the path you now travel. Yet, you do not believe God is here because you, in your infinite wisdom, have decided that we have interpreted God's Word incorrectly. You are both a hypocrite and a heretic."

"You're wrong!" Jacob said, "I didn't decide not to search on this path, because I think you're wrong or that I couldn't find God here. I assumed there would be no chance for open discussion, since everyone on this path is adamant they're right about God. Not everyone can be right, isn't that true?"

Campbell hesitated before responding sharply, "You have wasted enough of our time Mr. Hinsen. However, I've reviewed our files on you and it appears that you have never made a commitment to God, never! I'm not sure if you're searching to find God, or looking for reasons not to find Him."

Jacob wanted to disagree, but he wasn't sure Campbell's comments were incorrect. Was he searching for God because he knew He existed, or was his journey to prove he couldn't find Him, therefore God must not exist? Jacob did not know if he was more upset with Campbell for raising the questions or with himself for not asking them before.

"God is here, Hinsen, and I believe the worst punishment for you is realizing you have lost Him. You are lost in a quagmire of disbelief that will haunt you your entire life, and punish you in the next. Your punishment therefore is postponed. You are free to go, but remember to us you remain a heretic. Should you ever travel on our most Holy Path again, you will be punished in accordance to the Laws of God, as we have interpreted them. Go now, before I change my mind.

For hours after his release, Jacob shuddered each time he

recalled his encounter with Campbell and his men. His doubts and unanswered questions left him more confused then ever. When he began his journey, his plan had been to question others about why God is with them, and not other religions.

However, after his incident with Campbell the questions had been turned back to him; what do I believe? Who the hell is right, and how will I know?   As his anxiety subsided, Jacob was able to accept he did not have all the answers, and finding them was the essential reason for his journey.

The Path of Protestants has over 800 million travelers on it, almost as many as the Path of Roman Catholicism. Glancing down the Path, Jacob could see many smaller paths twisting off in different directions. Their symbols indicated who followed which path: Pentecostals, Baptists, Methodists, Anglicans, Lutherans, Jehovah's Witnesses, Mennonites, Church of Christ, Church of England, Amish, Episcopal, Mormons, Presbyterians, Seventh-Day Adventists, Quakers, Apostolic, and many more.

Jacob was feeling overwhelmed by the number of paths, so decided to take a breather at a local restaurant where he could review his maps and notes. He found a small eatery on the corner of the Path of Protestants and Mormon Way, and was surprised when the front door closed and locked behind him. No! He thought. Not a Fundamentalist restaurant!

"Don't be alarmed," a soft voice said. "There's no need to go back the way you came in. When you leave, you will exit through the far door, to the only path a person needs to follow."

"Is that right?" Jacob replied.

"Yes." said the voice said. "Will you be joining us for lunch in our dining area, or on our patio?"

Jacob explained he would not be eating, that he only wanted a cold glass of water with a twist of lemon.

"No problem at all," the waitress, whose name was Abigail (Abby) Penny said, "Why don't you have a seat at the table nearest the door and I'll bring you a pitcher of water."

"Thanks," Jacob responded, and took his seat. When she returned, he asked her to explain her earlier statement; "… only path a person needs to follow."

With a sweet smile, which seemed to say 'I got ya,' she explained.

"Like you, many who come by way of the Path of Protestants have a bulging and dusty backpack. Usually, this means the person is in search of God. I assumed you are one of those travelers."

"And where does the door you mentioned lead?"

"Oh! It will place you on Mormon Way, which is the only path to finding God."

He chuckled, "Well, you are right I'm a traveler on a quest to find God."

Jacob asked, "Abby is your faith strong enough for me to ask you about it without making you doubt your beliefs?"

"It is." Abby replied. "Nothing you ask will change my beliefs."

"Great!" Without wasting any time, Jacob said. "One of the problems I have with religion is with questions about the authenticity and accuracy of scriptures transcribed thousands, or in the case of Mormons a few decades ago. I understand the Mormon faith is based on the visions of a fourteen year old teenager in upstate New York who claimed to find hieroglyphic type messages from God. With the assistance of the Angel Moroni he translated the scriptures into the Book of Mormon, before the messages were lost. Which, if I understand your church's beliefs, supersedes all other Christian scripture. Is that right?"

"Correct!" Abby answered without discussion.

Jacob was taken back by Abby's composure and one word answer. Although he did not want to pass judgment on any religion, he did wonder how she was able to accept these beliefs. After all, the idea of a teenager getting a call from God, secret tablets, angels, and then the loss of the secret tablets, seemed pretty far-fetched to him. He continued.

"The initial writings of Mormon scripture, including the Book of Mormon, are attributed to Joseph Smith and his brother, Hyrum. Both were killed by a mob of non-Mormons who thought polygamy and other Mormon beliefs were sacrilegious."

"Right." Abby said softly.

Abby spoke next. "Mormons believe that the New Testament Bibles were full of errors and that these errors were corrected by Joseph Smith in the Book of Mormon. We also follow the teachings and direction of Brigham Young, Ezra Taft Benson, and others, and additional revelations and teachings that have been included in the Book."

"So, the Book of Mormon does supercede previous Christian scripture?"

"Not all of them. We believe the Bible is the Word of God, except those parts translated incorrectly. We also believe the corrected interpretations were entered into the Book of Mormon, which is the true Word of God."

"You mean those parts of the Bible that Mormon men determined were translated incorrectly are corrected in the

Book?"

"I guess you could put it that way." Abby replied.

"Out of millions of Christians worldwide, why did God select Joseph Smith, as his messenger?" Jacob asked.

"That's a great question and one you'll have to ask God to answer. Seriously, I think it is similar to God's selection of Abraham, Moses, John the Baptist, and others. It was based on his integrity, faith, love and total commitment to God."

"It's true Jacob, we have different ideologies then other Christian faiths, but we do share essential beliefs. We believe in the same organization that existed in the first church - apostles, prophets, pastors' teachers, and evangelists. We believe in the gifts of tongues, prophecy, revelation, visions, healing, and the interpretation of tongues. And, of course, we believe and place our love in God, the Eternal Father, and in His Son, Jesus Christ, and in the Holy Ghost."

"So what's different?" Jacob asked.

"Well, we claim the privilege of worshipping Almighty God according to the dictates of our conscience, and allow everyone else the same privilege; we let them worship how, where, or what they may."

"You mean you don't scorn or kill people because they have a different view? Mormons are really tolerant of all other religions?"

"Absolutely! Why would we kill someone because they don't believe what we do? Don't get me wrong, we do believe ours is the only way to God, but it's not up to me to tell you how God handles those who have chosen different paths."

"Will the others go to a separate section of Heaven, or to Hell?" Jacob asked.

"I really don't know. That is another question for God to answer. Although we tolerate other religions, it doesn't mean we believe they will all be treated equally by God. The Book of Mormon 24:19 says: 'And we know, that all men must repent and believe in the name of Jesus Christ, and worship the Father in his name, and endure in faith on his name to the end, or they cannot be saved in the kingdom of God.'

"Thanks," Jacob smiled and responded. "Are there any other major differences between Mormons and other Christian groups?"

"Well, the most extreme difference is that we believe there are many Gods, that each of us has the ability to achieve Godhood, and that we can have spirit children who will pray to us, as we pray to Jesus. This is similar to what Jesus, who we think of as a brother, and God the Father have done before us."

"Wow! That's radical!" Jacob said in disbelief. Could Abby be right? Could we all be God?

Abby noticed the surprise in Jacob's eyes and said, "To some, it appears radical Jacob. Nevertheless, think about this: if Jesus Christ is our paradigm and brother, and if we live our lives striving to transcend our human faults until we achieve His Holiness, then why wouldn't we be rewarded by the Father as Jesus was?"

"I guess?" Jacob said, as he tried to rationalize the idea.

After all, who is he to question someone's belief?

"I've got to get back to work, but please, do me a favor. Do not prejudge my church based only on what I've told you today. Think about what we've discussed and let God lead you."

"Can't we have five more minutes, please?" Jacob was almost pleading with her.

"Okay, five minutes, Jacob."

"How do you know so much about the details of the Mormon faith?"

"My part-time role is restaurant owner, but my full-time obligation is as a teacher and student of Mormonism."

"I should have known. So, why aren't you Catholic, Methodist, Baptist, or something else?"

"I, too, have traveled the roads you now travel. When I did, I found the Mormon Church more tolerant to other faiths in recognizing God alone will make the final decision on each of us. This, along with the ability for me to transcend to God the Father, as Jesus did, opened my heart to the Mormon Church. It is my belief Jacob, and only God will decide if I have chosen correctly."

"But how can you be so certain?"

"Oh Jacob of little faith, you travel because you haven't found God in your heart, but when your heart tells you He is found, as mine has, then you must believe the commandments God has left for you. The rest will become evident by the love you receive from others, the tolerance you will feel for others, and the acceptance of who you are as you journey to be like Jesus."

"The short answer is, because it is written, Jacob."

"It is written," she repeated, as if making the point that she, too, had heard those words many times before.

They parted with a hug of friendship and, after he finished his last gulp of water, Abby led Jacob to the door in the back . Jacob thanked her profusely, and stepped through the door onto the sunlit path of Mormon Way.

The awe-inspiring Mormon temple towered before him. Jacob knew it had taken forty years to build and included six towers, each well over 200 feet high. The temple was also the home of the renowned Mormon Tabernacle Choir, a magnificent choir of voices singing harmoniously with a single purpose: to praise a loving God.

He smiled as he began walking back toward the Path of Protestants, wondering what it would be like if religions were as harmonious as the choir.

So far it seems that each religion I explored, Jacob wrote in his journal that night, shares a similar narrative about how it originated: a man received a vision or direct message from God, or an angel. The message is always that existing religions have screwed up and God has selected him to correct the errors and bring His people home.

Once corrected, previous interpretations of God's Word are obsolete or inaccurate. I'm pretty sure I'll find similar origin messages within other religions, but I won't know until my journey is complete. The one constant seems to be an agreement with how it began: God, then Noah, Abraham, and so on, as outlined in the Hebrew Scriptures.

When I travel the Road of Judaism, I'll ask if these three religions of Abraham all began with the Jews, why have the Christians and Muslims persecuted the Jews, as if they never existed or communicated with God?

I am troubled, however, in that while I am learning a great deal about different religions, the origin narrative of each faith remains the same. Should this continue how will I ever find God.

Jacob traveled for many days along the abundant Paths of Protestants, and spoke to countless ordained clerics and devoted parishioners who graciously shared their counsel and candid opinions about their faith. Thanks to their kindness, he filled two large binders of notes to help him decide on the path God wanted him to travel.

Jacob continued on the Path of Protestants until he came to the well-marked Junction of the Majority. Other travelers had told him it existed, but he'd never seen it himself. He was in awe of the colossal crossroads where clerics from the many mainline Protestant denominations flocked.

The Junction of the Majority was where Baptists, Anglicans, Methodists, Lutherans, Episcopalians, Disciples of Christ, Presbyterians, and other factions acknowledged each other's presence, but worked independently to assimilate their unique point of view.

Each clergy person worked diligently to assemble an ideology to be transported by loyal messengers to senior members of their respective congregations. Each added unique emphasis points for their flocks, and forwarded the modifications to pastors, deacons and other laymen who would then preach the tailored message to millions of devoted parishioners around the world.

It didn't end there, Jacob observed; the motivated parishioners transported the message, after adding a few tweaks of their own, to family, friends and any sinner who they thought needed Jesus Christ for their salvation. Jacob was amazed as he watched the action unfold.

Nevertheless, he had to keep moving toward the final Protestant path left to travel, the Path of Lutherans. This was the path where Martin Luther broke from the Roman Catholic Church over a dispute about the infallibility of the Pope. Jacob wasn't sure why, but he felt optimistic about this path. After all, Martin Luther challenged the hypocrisy of the Roman Catholic Church, and millions considered him correct and followed. Maybe this was the path to God?

So, Jacob thought with a broad smile on his face, it looked as if he was off to see a Lutheran, an ordained Lutheran, of course. As he walked, he began to sing a tune he remembered from one of his favorite movies, the Wizard of Oz: 'I'm off to see a Lutheran, a wonderful Lutheran of course, because, because, because, because, because of the wonderful things they do.' He continued singing and whistling the tune for several blocks, and skipping to the tempo as Dorothy, the Tin Man and the Munchkins had done in the movie.

Located at 2342 Thoroughfare of Lutherans is a massive cathedral that beckons lost souls and loyal parishioners to enter its magnificent house of God. Jacob was astonished as he beheld the ancient building that seemed to reach into the heavens. It was comparable in grandeur to any of the opulent cathedrals he had noticed along the Path of Roman Catholicism.

The cathedral was the parish seat of the Reverend William Gillette, a prominent Lutheran spiritual leader. Gillette's Sunday sermons, his notes reminded him, are seen on live television stations by millions each week. Jacob felt honored that such a renowned Protestant leader had agreed to meet with him. He saw this as either a tremendous stroke of luck or divine intervention. Either way, he thanked God for the opportunity, and began fumbling through his notes for the questions he wanted to ask.

Damn! Jacob thought, as he suddenly began to feel overwhelmed. He wasn't sure if his excitement was because Reverend Gillette was so well known as a celebrity, or because he had the power to influence millions of people with his teachings. He made a mental note not to surrender to the Reverend's charisma, or ideology.

Facing the massive oak doors of the cathedral's offices, Jacob extended his finger and depressed the gold filigree doorbell.

He immediately heard the beautiful harmony of the chimes ringing out and took a moment to absorb the feelings of tranquility. He did not wait long for his feelings of tranquility to be replaced with the thrill of anticipation.

William Gillette stood before him, dressed in casual, albeit expensive, clothes. He extended his hand in welcome. "Come in, young man," he said with a cheerful voice. "You must be the traveler I have heard about? Come in, I believe we have a great deal to talk about."

Within minutes, it was obvious to Jacob the charismatic champion of God knew how to captivate his guests. Reverend Gillette exuded confidence, so much that Jacob feared he might be too overwhelmed to ask him any questions for fear of appearing dumb. On the other hand, the honesty and sincerity radiating from Gillette's eyes revealed his love for people, God, and, as Jacob would learn, an inner patience when answering "dumb" questions.

As they settled themselves in Reverend Gillette's office,

which to Jacob felt more like the lobby of a grand hotel, Gillette asked him to begin when he was ready. "No rush," the Reverend added, "I've left plenty of time for our meeting."

Jacob wasted no time starting. "Reverend Gillette, seeing your magnificent office makes me wonder, how do you feel about the notion that the rich will not enter the Kingdom of Heaven? Sir, how do you respond to that question? Obviously, you and your church are rich."

Gillette laughed politely, indicating he had heard the question many times. "Jacob," he said, "I believe that only happens when people place the power of money and riches before their love for God and others.

"And," he continued, "why would God want man to be without the possessions He has given man the ability to create? Take, for instance, the magnificent discoveries in modern medicine, education, science, and technology. Many people living in poverty are not able to take advantage of these great achievements. Therefore, I do not believe God wants some of His people to live in poverty, surrender to illiteracy, suffer through famine, or be dependent on others."

"No, Jacob, in my humble belief, God's plan for humankind does not endorse a poverty philosophy. However, it does not support a welfare state either. That is, people must work towards improving themselves, their love for others, their environment, and most of all their love for Jesus Christ. When they do, God will give them all the rewards in this life they will ever need."

"But, what about those who are rich?"

"Those who believe in the Lord and have gained wealth are obligated through their love as Christians to help those who are less fortunate. They will enter Heaven. Those who are rich without the Lord, and who neglect those in need for selfish or prejudiced reasons, will not."

"My belief is that if everyone had access to the great advancements God has provided man, then jealousy, contempt for other's faiths, hatred, and the divisions between rich and poor would be minimized. Does this answer your question?"

"I understand, thank you," Jacob replied. "Would you be kind enough to explain a little about Martin Luther and his split from the Catholic Church?"

"My pleasure. The condensed version is this: "Martin Luther was ordained in 1507 as an Augustinian Monk, and, in 1521 was excommunicated for teachings that were contradictory to Roman Catholic doctrine. His famous Ninety-five Theses challenged the authority of the Pope to bestow indulgences."

"Indulgences?" Jacob asked, "I'm not sure I understand the meaning."

"Indulgences were when a rich person paid a fee to the Pope to forgive the sins of someone who died, and who they suspected was suspended in purgatory."

"Purgatory," Jacob interrupted, "is the holding space between Heaven and Hell for sinners who must repent and do good works before they can ascend to Heaven or descend into Hell." Jacob hoped there was a holding space between Heaven and Hell, especially on account of his confusion over religion, and the number of journeys he'd initiated to find God. If he screwed up by not choosing a faith to follow, at least he might have a second chance.

"Good enough, Jacob." Reverend Gillette continued. "Through indulgences, the Pope authorized himself to forgive sins, but Martin Luther believed this was an abuse of authority, since only Jesus can forgive sins."

Reverend Gillette went on to explain how Luther's challenges led to the great schism between Protestants and Roman Catholics later known as the Reformation. The main differences between ideologies, as outlined by Martin Luther, is that Protestants believe salvation comes through faith alone, and not good works; Jesus Christ alone can forgive sins, not the pope, priest, or any other man; there are but two sacraments, not seven (baptism and the Eucharist); that Jesus is merely symbolic in the Eucharist; and the Bible, and not the Pope is the final Word of God."

"So, then, who's right Catholics or Protestants?" Jacob asked.

"I like that Jacob, direct questions." Gillette paused for a moment before continuing, "My short answer, of course, would be the Protestants are. That's why I am a Lutheran. However, as we discuss the differences, it will also help to explain my position."

"Makes sense to me." Jacob said.

Over the next several hours, Jacob probed Gillette's convictions on many of the same topics of authenticity and scriptural fallibility he had discussed with Father Doyle, Cardinal

Leopold, Abby, and other clerics. Although Gillette shared new details and opinions, overall the explanation was the same: "It is written."

As he became more comfortable with his new understanding of Lutheran beliefs, Jacob moved from questions regarding interpretations of scripture, and who is right, to specific ones about Christian leadership that had long lingered in his mind.

"Reverend Gillette," Jacob asked. "You said that Martin Luther had valid reasons for being disenchanted with the Pope and the direction the Roman Catholic Church was taking. Nevertheless, in Luther's Ninety-five Theses he mentioned no compelling disagreements with the direction Christianity had taken since the teachings, crucifixion, and resurrection of Jesus Christ."

"So, let me agree the New Testament, as translated from Greek to German by Martin Luther, was factual. That is, no person ever changed a word or phrase."

Reverend Gillette nodded.

"Let's also agree that all Christians acknowledge Jesus Christ as the Savior, and that His teachings were of love, kindness, and tolerance for all mankind. Not murder, world domination, or spreading the Good News through wars or condemnation."

"Agreed." Reverend Gillette replied.

"My questions are: why didn't Luther or other prominent leaders demand a change to the way Christianity had moved from Jesus' teachings of love and tolerance, to the destructive power of religion through wars and persecution?"

"Why did reformers focus more on indulgences than on changing the philosophy that justified the devastation sanctioned by the Crusades, or the horrific inquisitions carried out in Jesus' name? And where were the reformers when at least ten Popes, and numerous Cardinals, were known to be corrupt, adulterous and, in a couple of instances, murderers?"

"For my benefit let me clarify your questions," Gillette replied, "which pertain to why Christian reformers seemed more interested in debating the essence of Jesus or the inconsistencies of scriptures and ideologies, instead of the issue of why Christianity began contradicting the teachings of Jesus?"

"Yes!" Jacob replied. "It seems that scriptures which teach the peaceful messages of Jesus are used to explain how we should live individually. While the brutality of God's wrath drawn from the Hebrew scriptures is used by the Church to justify wars, consent to cruel and unjust punishment, sanction ethnic cleansing, and retain supremacy over the same parishioners whom they have told to 'love thy neighbor.' "

"Let it all out, Jacob. You have anger in your heart that needs to be released."

"I guess I do, Reverend. I don't understand why Catholics slaughter Protestants, Protestants murder Catholics, Christians hate and kill Muslims, Muslims hate and kill Jews and Christians, Jews kill Muslims and probably Christians and then justify it as following the teachings of the same God!"

"I understand the anguish in your heart, and it's not unjustified, in many cases." Reverend Gillette replied. "Let me answer your questions in the same way I've helped others to understand why our actions so often conflict with the teachings of Jesus. I'll tell you what is in my heart, rather than direct you to specific scriptures, since I'm sure you've already covered all the scriptures you need."

Jacob nodded in agreement.

"The first thing you need to understand is that no one has the answers to all of your questions except God. Nevertheless, I will try to help you with your inner struggle. Jesus Christ is perfect humankind is not. Period! As hard as we may try, none of us is close to Jesus' perfection. No human is immune to the temptation of sin or evil acts. Jesus understood we would fall, thrash about, and succumb to human biases. Unfortunately, we have not disappointed Him on this."

"Let me rephrase that, we have disappointed Him, but Jesus knew we would need time to grow from the Old Biblical teachings to those of the New Testament. Hell! The Apostles had doubts and some walked and talked with Him themselves. Thank goodness God has more patience than Man," he said, chuckling.

"Jacob, I will not attempt to justify the atrocities you referenced. Many people were and are today corrupt and lust for power. Men succumb to evil, even religious men with the best intentions. But do not discount the many more Christians who have devoted themselves to Jesus with a mission to elevate ancient tribal mentalities, to a Jesus-way of thinking. We have a long way to go before we walk the walk of Jesus, but we cannot let mistakes of our past, present and future allow us to languish in our attempts to achieve peace and salvation through the teachings of Jesus Christ."

Jacob was impressed with the reverend's strong convictions. His mastery of vocalization made every statement thought provoking or accepted as truth. He felt how easy it was to be drawn to Reverend's convictions.

Gillette spoke again, "I promise Jacob, this is not a sermon!"

Jacob laughed, and Reverend Gillette continued.

"Since the beginning of time, mankind has rebelled against God, and been influenced by worldly self-indulgence. As man strayed further from God, church leaders such Martin Luther stepped forward in an attempt to bring them back. The Reformation was successful because Luther's message was accepted by many Christians, now called Protestants, who believed the changes he called for would return them to the true Path of God."

"But I still don't understand. If the new message doesn't bring you back to the kindness taught by Jesus, how do you separate the old from the new?" Jacob asked.

"Good question. I believe that ideologies grow in the same way we grow as individuals. That is, our belief grows through our personal trials and errors, not because we simply say we accept Jesus in our hearts. We are bombarded each day with outside influences, good and bad, which we must learn to overcome. We fail more times than we succeed, but we will eventually win if our efforts are pure and focused towards one objective, God.

The same is true of religion. The people struggling to reach God are the same ones reforming religion. Many great religious leaders were not pure, kind hearted, or as enlightened as Jesus would have wanted. For all the good teachings of Martin Luther, he was regarded as a difficult person to get along with and didn't always teach in accordance with Jesus' instructions."

"What do you mean?" Jacob asked.

"For instance, he preached fierce anti-Semitism. It's deplorable how hate became a part of religious ideology by good people, and then went on to fuel territorial and tribal disputes for thousands of years."

"We tend not to turn the other cheek, as Jesus taught." Jacob added; "thereby, religions' crusade against each other and the winner's interpretation of scriptures becomes the ideology people must follow."

"Well," Gillette replied cautiously, "it's not as simple as that, but when you look at religions history, it has happened. Yet keep in mind, change of this magnitude is a long journey. We can only strive to change what we can in our short lifetime. God will judge each of us accordingly."

It was late, and Jacob had taken a great deal of the reverend's time. "Reverend Gillette, you've given me a wonderful day of conversation that I will not forget. Your sincerity, candor, and patience in answering my questions has been tremendously helpful."

"Thank you, Jacob," he replied warmly. "I've enjoyed myself, too. But I'm not sure I answered all your questions. I can tell you this: my belief in Jesus Christ is what guides me even when I am unable to understand His actions. We all struggle; we all have dark sides, yet through our faith we can endeavor to reach God's realm of kindness, love and acceptance. We are not there yet, but do not give up on us, we'll make it. All of us will," he emphasized.

Jacob believed him.

As they made their way to the door, Jacob reminded Reverend Gillette that he'd almost forgotten the final question of the night. The Reverend paused for a moment and said, "Ah, yes, whose ideologies are correct, the Catholics or Protestants?"

"Great memory," Jacob said smiling.

"First, both doctrines believe in Jesus Christ, which is Christianity's most important building block. The remaining building blocks I give to the Lutherans, though I know not all Protestants or Catholics would agree with me. That's my final answer, Jacob."

"Logical," Jacob replied, "and diplomatic for sure. But how are you sure?"

Smiling and staring into Jacob's eyes, he replied; "Because, it is written, Jacob! Because it is written."

They bid each other farewell, and as the great door closed behind him, Jacob marveled at hearing the same words again, "It is written."

As he stood on the Thoroughfare of Lutherans Jacob knew he had to leave the Road of Christianity in search of other paths. He felt uneasy that God had not yet revealed Himself. And for the first time, he was aware of the possibility that he might never return to this great Road again; the one he had spent his entire life traveling.

CONFRONTATION WITH DOUBT

Time's a wasting, Jacob said to himself as he pulled the compass from his backpack to confirm his directions. He would soon be traveling on the Road of Islam.

The Road of Islam presented a significant challenge to Jacob. It was as large as Christianity's, but he was not as familiar with the Islamic faith. What little he did know concerned him. As experienced by millions of others, Islamic Fundamentalism was thrust upon him on September 11, 2001, when nearly three thousand people were killed in New York City by a group of Islamic terrorists who flew two commercial planes into the World Trade Center.

The event continued to haunt him. He remained baffled as to why religious fanatics believe Allah, the same God worshiped by Christians and Jews, blessed the atrocity that killed innocent Muslims, Jews, Christians, and countless others. He had to find God for the answer.

Several hours passed before Jacob felt comfortable on the path he now traveled to Islam. The people were cordial in passing, some even waved, but for the most part they remained focused on whatever it was they were already doing. He was relieved, that he did not seem to be on another path of Fundamentalists.

In spite of the pleasant atmosphere, Jacob had a bizarre feeling that something was different. There was nothing specific he could put his finger on, it was just one of those intuitive feelings, he guessed. Yet, why now? He knew he was heading in the right direction, but then realized he had never seen a name sign for the path he was traveling. He decided it was a good chance to stop to get something to eat, and check his route to determine if the path was one of Christianity, Judaism, Islam, or all three.

The tavern was similar to many others. Inside was a large bar encircled by high backed stools, which held a few loyal patrons. There was a small dining room adjacent to the room. Jacob chose the stool that gave him the best view of the room while also keeping his back to the wall, an old combat habit he'd picked up in the Marines to ensure no one could sneak up behind him.

He ordered a draft beer from the melancholy bartender and looked around to see if anyone appeared like they wanted to talk. Only one man appeared friendly and approachable. He was dressed in a blue suit and was reading a financial newspaper.

"Excuse me, Sir, I don't mean to interrupt you, but I've been traveling east from The Road of Christianity toward The Road of Islam, and I was wondering if you had a couple of minutes to answer a few questions for me? I'm looking for answers about some of the beliefs of the people along this passage."

"Beliefs?" the man replied, folding his paper and putting it on the far end of the table, "What kind of beliefs? Regardless, I have time to talk about anything you like, but I'm not sure 'belief' is the operative word here." Jacob didn't know what the man's last remark was leading to, but he'd obviously selected a person who wanted to talk.

The man motioned for Jacob to join him. As he did, the man removed his suit jacket and placed it on the back of the chair beside him. Great, Jacob thought, this is going to be an interesting conversation! He dearly hoped, however, what seemed to be the man's fascination with his own intelligence wouldn't interfere with them having a good conversation.

Jacob learned the man's name was Arnold Robust, and that he enjoyed talking to travelers. Jacob summarized his search to find God, where he'd been, and where he was headed. Arnold seemed interested, which made Jacob wonder if he once might have made the same journey himself.

"You're heading in the right direction to reach The Road of Islam. It's about two days from here." Damn, Jacob thought, it looked closer than that. Arnold continued and asked; "When you reach the Road, what are you expecting to find?"

"I want to know it it's the path to finding God," Jacob answered. He thought he had already explained this to Arnold.

"And what if it is not? What if there is no God?" Arnold asked, carefully emphasizing each word.

Jacob told him "No God" was not an option for him. He wanted to believe God existed, but needed to find the true path to ensure that he reached Him.

"But what if there is no God?" Arnold repeated. "What if you find no proof that God exists anywhere, and that the only life you have is the one you are living today? What if…?"

"What if what, Arnold? Jacob interrupted. "What if God is lost, or I find that the only life we have begins at birth and ends with death? I've told you I choose to think there is a God."

"Why?"

"I told you. I'm on a quest to find Him to answer my questions. Until I find otherwise, my belief is God exists."

"No, no Jacob," Arnold responded firmly, "What you are telling me is that you have no doubt there is a God, but that you simply need to know which path will take you to Him. However, my question to you has been, how do you know there is a God? Because, if there is no God, then it doesn't matter which path you take, does it?"

Jacob could tell Arnold was attempting to control the direction of the conversation and responded, "I'm short on time, so can I please ask you something else before we get sidetracked by the mysteries of life?

"Could you please tell me the name of the path here? I've seen no road signs, it's not on my maps, and frankly, I'm not sure this path that pertains to my quest at all."

"I've challenged you with my questions about God," Arnold said, "because I've have traveled the same roads and paths you travel now. The majority of people you will meet on this path have also traveled many of the same roads, and all of them became lost in the chaos of religion.

"You asked me several times for the name of the path you now travel, but those of us who travel it have decided it doesn't really need a name. This isn't because it's less of a path than the others. More accurately, it's an integral characteristic of them all. It often appears less traveled than other paths, yet more and more travelers join us every day because we accept only the truth."

Jacob still did not know where Arnold was heading with this, but he let him continue without interruption.

"If we named the path, chances are you and the others would prefer not to travel here for fear of being tainted by the logic of our beliefs. Like you, all of us here have been burdened by the same unanswered questions, doubt and confusion as to what is believable. The only difference between you and us is that we do not share your belief in God. This in itself doesn't make us bad people, because no group is all good or all bad. To this end, we are like believers of any religious denomination."

"So you do have some sort of religious belief?" Jacob asked, perhaps a little impatiently. After all, he still had no straight answer about the name of the path.

Arnold sensed the agitation in Jacob's voice, but continued.

"Our belief, Jacob, is in today and in pure reason. That is, each day is lived with the realization there may not be a tomorrow. If I were to name the path you are traveling, I guess I would call it The Path of-"

"Wait!" Jacob interrupted, "am I on The Path of Atheists? Is that why you didn't tell me its name sooner?" Jacob wasn't mad at Arnold, but he was furious with himself for not recognizing the path before he'd engaged in a conversation there.

"I understand the position you're in," Arnold said, "and, as I mentioned to you earlier, many of us have traveled the same roads you travel now and have reached the conclusion that this path is as good, if not better, than the others.

"We believe it is the Road of Existence and Reality, not the 'Road of Disbelief,' because our belief is in today and, with luck, tomorrow. We don't believe in life after death or God. What happens to us in this life is purely by chance and is subject to reason. Our world and universe is in constant chaos, and the happenstances of our lives are random, not planned by supernatural intervention."

"How can you think that?" Jacob asked, "Just hearing you talk makes me think of a lonely and sad existence. How do you 'know' there's no God, or afterlife?"

"Because the biblical stories are not logical" Arnold snapped. "Come on Jacob, you're a smart guy, is there really any logic to the contradictions religion expects you to accept."

"Arnold," Jacob argued, "you're looking at the world from man's logic. Do you think man is the most intelligent being in the universe? Today's logic is often superseded by tomorrow's discoveries. Why do you think we have the ability to understand what the universe holds for us?"

"That was a religious answer, Jacob. Yes, our way can seem lonely to outsiders, but do you believe in God and Heaven because you don't want to be alone, or because you fear the alternative: that life on earth is absolute, ashes to ashes, dust to dust, period?"

Arnold was on a roll, but at this point Jacob was blocking out what he was saying. Nothing he was saying was new to Jacob, the doubt, confusion and inability to prove empirically the foundations of belief had been an internal conflict of his throughout his life. The only answers he'd ever been given were "Because it is written," or "I believe there is a God, therefore you must believe in God," or the best of all, "God works in mysterious ways." These ambiguous answers weren't ones Jacob supported, nor ones he wanted to use against Arnold's arguments.

Jacob went on offensive. "You speak against religion, but as an atheist you hold your ideology as sacred as any religion's. Your religion is simply not believing in God!"

Arnold snapped back again, "We are not a religion."

Jacob did not back down. "As an Atheist you can't deny your mission. It's not to live peacefully in your own beliefs; it's to convert people to your way of thinking, and you consider those who don't share your unbelief ignorant. You pursue logic the same way Christians and Muslims pursue converts to God."

"But you never hear us attributing senseless wars and murder to a God!" Arnold argued.

"No, not to God, but man's logic is used by atheists like Josef Stalin to achieve the same results. I don't try to answer for everyone Arnold, but I choose to believe there is a higher power. The problem I have with atheists and religious fundamentalists is their absolute conviction they are right, and everyone else is wrong."

In his own way, Arnold was looking for answers to the same questions Jacob was. Both were searching for the truth, for proof, and without proof, the only answers they had were what they chose to believe. Was it that simple?

By now he was confused and tired of arguing about questions no one had answers to. Arnold or science cannot explain where the atom of energy came from that started the Big Bang. Or, for that matter, what created the empty void, we call space that the Bang expanded in to. More speculation, he thought. He had to find God. Only then would he have the true answers.

Jacob rose slowly from his seat and politely interrupted Arnold, shook his hand, thanked him for his time and perspective, and said good-bye. As he started to leave Arnold spoke in a loud, yet surprisingly sincere voice.

"Thank you, Jacob. If you do find proof God exists, please come back and tell me!" The other atheists at the bar chuckled, but Jacob had a feeling Arnold wasn't joking.

Outside, Jacob headed directly toward The Road of Islam, deciding he would not stop until he reached it.

Thinking back, Jacob hoped he hadn't been too rude to Arnold. After all, he was a man of conviction who simply tried to convince him why his beliefs were the logical truth. Frustrated, Jacob wondered why there only seemed to be one way.

THE ROAD OF ISLAM

After two days of almost non-stop traveling, Jacob finally reached the Road of Islam. As he did before beginning his travels on previous paths, he reviewed his notes so not to be totally ignorant of the what to expect.

Let me see, he said to himself, Muslims believe the Quran is the last testament given to mankind by God, and that it represents God's directives, in Arabic, as given to the Prophet Muhammad over a twenty-three year period. Muhammad recorded everything exactly as God directed, which ensures the Quran is infallible. Unlike Christian believers, Muslims recognize no intermediate divine beings, as Jesus. They do recognize "great prophets," a group to which they believe Jesus belongs.

The Road of Islam was almost as massive as the Road of Christianity; devoted followers numbering 1.4 billion. It too, was very impressive. As with Christianity, there are many paths open to Muslims, depending on their interpretation of Allah's Word.

From his vantage point Jacob could see many of these paths, those of the Sunni and Shi'a (or Shi'ite), and their subsidiaries, including Wahhabis, Sufis, Fakir, Druze, Zaidis, Black Muslims, Marabouts, and several more.

The grandeur of Islam was evident from the magnificent palaces of the rich, to the beautiful mosques, Islam's holy places of worship. The most celebrated mosques, like Masjid al-Haram, Masjid Nabawi, and Cordoba, could be seen from where he stood, as could the most sacred of all Islamic sites, the Mosques of Madina, Maccah, and the Dome of the Rock.

Jacob knew mosques were more significant in Muslims' daily lives, and that they were used in conjunction with the five daily prayers. He also knew prayer halls held no seats, images, sculptures, or ritual objects. All face east, towards Mecca.

He would soon learn that mosques are nondenominational; a Muslim adherent may pray in any mosque. Mosques also serve as community centers for religious events, education, and courts of law; some even have parade grounds, libraries, hospitals or other facilities.

Also visible, however, was the poverty, illiteracy, disease, prejudice and bondage of people confined to a standard of living unchanged for thousands of years. Standards enforced by religious and secular leaders.

"Excuse me sir," Jacob called out to a man nearby, "I'm looking for The Path of the Sunni, can you help me?" He decided to follow this path first, simply because it was the largest in Islam. The man nodded his head, smiled and pointed to the wide road that veered off to Jacob's left.

The Path of Sunni was as large, if not larger, than the Path of Roman Catholicism. Of the 1.4 billion Muslims around the world, the Sunni accounted for almost eighty five percent.

He was anxious to begin, but first located an envelope in his backpack that had been given to him by an old college friend, Jerry Staffert. Staffert was a professor of International Affairs at the University of New York, and had agreed to give Jacob some background information about people he might want to contact on the Road of Islam.

Having received the note just before he left home, he had put it in his backpack without reading it. Looking at it now for the first time he was surprised, knowing Jerry's thoroughness, it only included the name of one scholar, Muhja.

There was nothing to indicate if Muhja was a first or last name, or perhaps even a full name? Luckily, Jerry noted Muhja could be found in a small mosque located at the corner of Haashir and Waheed Lanes, researching religions of the world.

Soon Jacob was standing before the small mosque. There were only a few people talking outside the main entrance, so he decided to ask them to help him locate Muhja.

"Excuse me," Jacob said to three men sitting at a small table, "I apologize for interrupting you, but I am looking for Mr. Muhja."

One replied chuckling, "Good evening, my name is Rasool Ra'ahah, I know Muhja, whom you almost certainly will find in the library inside."

"Thank you," Jacob responded. "Do I need to remove my shoes?"

"It's obvious to us that you are a traveler, and know little about the path you now travel, but that's not a problem; we are all travelers in our own way. As for your question, you may enter and pray in shoes, but it would show respect if you did as we do and removed them to avoid soiling the carpet."

As Jacob turned and proceeded toward the library, he wondered why the men chuckled when he asked for Mr. Muhja. He assumed it was his incorrect pronunciation.

Upon entering a mosque for the first time, Jacob was impressed with the simple, natural elegance of its interior. Verses of the Quran were written on the corridor walls in Arabic, with English translations underneath. Each verse inscribed with great precision. He noticed people gathered throughout the building in small discussion groups and several others in deep meditation or prayer.

As he entered the library Jacob noticed the books seemed to have worn bindings or protruding page markers, which suggested to him they had been well read. He looked around for a librarian who might help him locate Muhja, but saw no one.

Just as he was about to begin asking those he saw reading, he noticed a man shelving books. He walked quietly toward him.

The man told him he would find Muhja behind a stack of books, at the far corner table.

Jacob thanked the librarian and made his way to the table. No one was there, but Jacob decided to wait.

Over the next twenty minutes, several men passed by, yet none took a seat at the table. Finally, a mature Asian woman of fair appearance stepped from behind one of the large stacks holding an armful of manuscripts.

"Excuse me," Jacob said smiling; "I am looking for Muhja and was told he usually works at this table."

The woman set the manuscripts down and replied softly, "Yes, I am familiar with Muhja, who is a great scholar of the laws and traditions of Islam and other religions. In fact, I think Muhja is the most unique scholar in the world, and if you are privileged to spend time with Muhja I suggest you listen carefully and take many notes."

"Wonderful," Jacob said. "Thank you. I'll wait here for as long as it takes him to return."

The woman laughed and extended her hand to shake Jacob's saying, "Good evening, I am Muhja."

After the hot flash of embarrassment drained from his face, Jacob laughed and thought to himself, so much for first impressions. "You know, Muhja," he said; "I have never been set up so perfectly, nor felt so ill prepared. I was referred to you by Jerry Staffert, a name she quickly acknowledged.

Please forgive me for thinking you would be a man, but I thought all Islamic scholars were men?"

"Most are, yes, but as you see not all. As you say in the West, 'we've come a long way, baby!" She then turned business like and said; "Please sit down."

"Thank you."

Muhja put away her paperwork, closed her books, and turned to Jacob. "Jacob, I am now devoted to our conversation. I will offer you whatever assistance I can. I do use the word "God" interchangeably with "Allah," so do not be confused. As a bit of information, Islam has over ninety glorious names with which we refer to God.

"First, why don't you bring me up to date on what you've learned on your travels and what you think I can help you with during our discussion."

Muhja struck Jacob as a woman who would enjoy a good debate. He admired the way she got right to the heart of the discussion, and even more, her non-confrontational manner and sense of humor.

"Agreed!" Jacob responded, and began to talk to her non-stop about his quest, the people he had spoken to, and the paths he still had to travel. He also explained his dilemma with scripture, the conflicting roads of religion, and his difficulty in understanding the true meaning of a loving God.

Muhja sat silently, making notes, nodding occasionally, and offering a few smiles and frowns in response to the comments he was making.

Jacob could not believe how much he was babbling, it

was as if his mind was a dam and someone had opened the valves. As he finished Muhja set down her pen, folded her arms, and looked him straight in the eye.

"I'm proud of you, Jacob. Not many people would endure the journey you have undertaken. Some because they are committed to the doctrine they were taught to accept, many simply find comfort in uniting with what the majority believe, still others do not care, or find solace in whatever path is simplest for them. You have ventured upon this Path in search of truth, but I must tell you with all sincerity I may only have the truth as I perceive it."

"I'm not sure I understand what you mean, Muhja?"

"What I mean is the personal truth I give to you is the truth I've acquired over years of intense study and deliberation with scholars of Islam and other religions. Even with this knowledge it is possible I may not have the answers to your questions. Do you understand?"

"Absolutely. I am grateful to you for meeting with me. I respect your credentials and above all your honesty and integrity. So, where do we begin?" Before she could answer, he continued enthusiastically,

"I have a lot of questions."

"I would suggest I begin by clarifying for you many of the common misconceptions about Islam. Once you understand these, you will be able to understand the broader context of Islam. It is a simple approach that I think may work well for us. Okay?" She rhetorically asked.

"I'm sure you have found in your travels, Jacob, that different religions have different scriptures, opinions, biases, and interpretations of God's Word."

Jacob nodded and thought to himself; that's an understatement.

"Even with all of the phenomenal advancements in technology, and especially communication, people do not always get the entire story on every topic. The advent of the Internet is proof in point: individuals with only minimal knowledge can post information as if they were scholars in any field. People don't take the time to validate each message, and so half-truths can spread."

Like religion? Jacob thought to himself; knowing from experience it was all about the message, how the information was presented, and by whom often determined people's acceptance of an idea.

Jacob wondered it Muhja was really an independent thinker or is she was about to extol the virtues of Islam versus the corruption of the West and its media.

"For that matter," Muhja was saying, "information is often conveyed to boost ratings, or give customers partial news that the media assumes their customers want to hear. On a less frequent, yet more malicious basis, the media communicate messages only the media wants people to hear."

"But Muhja that is exactly what is happening in countries around the world where leaders control the news so their people hear only what they want them to hear. This is happening today in Iraq, Iran, North Korea, and other places," Jacob responded.

"Don't get me wrong, Jacob," She interjected. "I'm not

condemning technology, rather I oppose the governments, religious leaders, and profiteers who manipulate the media for personal reasons and to show the worst of man's behavior, especially as it pertains to Islam."

Okay Jacob thought. He understood the connection Muhja was making between the modern media and the spread of misconceptions about Islam, but this wasn't what he'd traveled so far to hear.

"With this in mind," Muhja was saying, "let me give tell you of one misconception about Islam and Muslims in general. We are not all extremists, fundamentalists or terrorists."

Muhja's comments so far reinforced Jacob's confidence that she wasn't trying to guide him down a one-way path. She was not only intelligent, but also interested in an open exchange of ideas.

"But would you agree, Muhja, that the greatest portion of violence against non-Muslims and Muslims alike is committed by Muslims who are not from rogue splinter groups, but are state-sponsored workers? They say do it in the name of Allah because they are taught Allah will reward them in Paradise, with lots of virgins."

Though he was asking his question of Muhja, he knew in his heart it was a question only God could answer.

"My point is whether the media reports it accurately or not, followers of Islam have been practicing these atrocities under the auspices of Allah for thousands of years."

"Unfortunately it has happened that way," Muhja admitted, "but it's not representative of all Muslims."

"Of course it isn't," Jacob agreed, "just as all Christians aren't Crusaders or Jews haters of Jesus Christ. I don't disagree with you that communication can be manipulated, but in all fairness there has been little counter-response by good Muslims to condemn those who use Allah to justify violence. Where is the counter-revolt against these fanatics by the peaceful followers of Islam?"

"You have valid points Jacob," Muhja said, "and as Muslims we must do more to demonstrate the kindness of the majority. Think about this though, when Irish Catholic groups kill Protestants, or innocent Muslims are killed by Orthodox Jewish militiamen, or Orthodox anti-Muslim groups massacre thousands of Muslims in the Baltics, the world doesn't condemn the entire Christian, Jewish, or Orthodox population, and rightfully so!"

"Islam is a religion of peace, and the majority of us live according to the peaceful teachings of Allah. The Quran clearly states, '[…if anyone slew a person … it would be as if he slew a whole people … (5.32)]' yet, because of a minority of fundamentalists, the majority of us must live in fear of retribution."

"I'm not disagreeing with you," Jacob said. He was ready to move the conversation to another topic, but couldn't resist asking one more question.

"Muhja, I appreciate your thoughts on the image of Islam and Muslims in general. On the other hand, it's hard for me to understand how Islam can call itself a peaceful way of life or religion. How do you account for the Taliban taking control of

Afghanistan and then killing, brutalizing and suppressing a nation of fellow Muslims? They claimed their actions were righteous and punishments distributed as God commanded in the Quran."

"One second," Muhja interrupted, "your understanding of the Taliban is not complete. This is an excellent example of people only knowing half the story, the half that made the news. At first, the Afghans perceived them as a group of warriors who offered change from the country's tribal lawlessness. The Taliban achieved success by eliminating corruption and restoring peace among tribal warlords. They were also instrumental in jump-starting Afghanistan's unstable economy, albeit at the expense of the population. I'm not telling you this to justify their methods," she continued, "I tell you this to demonstrate my point about what the world hears and is led to believe."

It was obvious Muhja was a proud Muslim and that misconceptions about her religion were a personal and emotional subject for her. Yet, as much as he wanted to agree with her and move on, Jacob also had to express his own views.

"Does it bother you, then, to see a strict interpretation of religious law used to control people of the same faith? Is that what a loving God really intended?"

"Yes, it bothers me when the codes of law are manipulated, and no I do not believe it is what Allah expects from us," Muhja answered.

"With all due respect," Jacob responded, "The twenty-first century was ushered in with the image of Muslim suicide bombers, targeted terrorist atrocities, and Islamic brutality."

"Fundamentalists," Muhja sharply interrupted; "We are back to fundamentalists."

"No, we're back to the world's perception of Islam, and, even more importantly, what the world would look like under the rule of a strict religious ideology. My true fear is not the bombers themselves, but the religious leaders who teach and guide them, telling the killers it is what God wants them to do."

"Jacob," she said calmly, "you make some good observations, not all of which I agree with, but enough to know we will not resolve their answers tonight. I brought up the topic of misconceptions first because of its importance to me as a Muslim, and because most travelers do not have the knowledge, you have demonstrated. Nevertheless, we are not here to debate or try to convince one or the other to change their beliefs. We are together tonight to exchange ideas, transfer knowledge, build a friendship and provide you with the knowledge of Islam you require to make your decision."

"However," she continued; "for my own personal pride and satisfaction, please allow me close this part of our conversation with a couple of things I truly want you to understand about Islam."

"You know Islam originated in Arabia and spread through the ancient Middle East primarily through war and bloodshed. This is similar to the expansion of other ancient religions, such as Judaism and Christianity. Nevertheless, what people don't understand is that Islam prospered and spread around the world under the teachings of peace and tolerance, not war."

"Furthermore, many people do not realize the majority of the world's Muslims live peacefully outside the Middle East. There are around 200 million Muslims in Indonesia alone, over

70 million in Russia, and millions more in Africa, China, and the West. More importantly," she emphasized, "Islam is not a religion in the same sense as Christianity; Islam is a complete way of life, a total submission to Allah and His word."

"I'm not sure I understand," Jacob said.

"My apologies, I may be getting ahead of myself," she replied. "Let me give you an example. Many Western countries have a clear separation of church and state. Islam, however, primarily follows Allah's Laws, and secular laws, when appropriate. True Muslims live their daily lives devoted to the Word of God, as instructed in the Quran, Sunnahs, and complementing scriptures."

"What are the Sunnahs?

"We'll get to that in more detail later as needed." She replied. "For now, let me simply say that Islamic law is made up of four principle sources, which together are called Sharia, and which serve as the total law for the people of Islam. First, of course, is the Quran, the infallible Word of God. Next is the Sunnah, the traditions and examples set by the Prophet Muhammad. Third is ijma, or decisions of the community, and the fourth is qiyas, or legal analogy.

"The Islamic system of law provides guidance for every endeavor a Muslim undertakes, such as marriage, obligations to God, ownership of property, even family planning and the raising of children. Islam is not political in a Western sense, but the Sharia is the complete social, economical, political and spiritual way of life. In Islam, there is no dispute between secular laws and God's Laws, since no law supersedes the Word of God, as commanded in the Quran."

"But, why Muhja?" Jacob asked confused.

"Why, what?" she responded, puzzled by the question.

"Why do people have to be led by the hand and limited to one ideology? Why must their lives be governed by men?"

"They are governed by the Word of Allah, Jacob," she replied softly.

"Yes." He responded; "But the Word of God has been interpreted so differently by clerics in all religions. Limitations established on what people can believe, strict religious laws, restrictions on personal discovery of other cultures, and ancient rituals which in many cases were directed to control masses of people thousands of years ago."

Muhja interrupted, "I am not sure I agree they hinder freedom of thought and personal discovery, especially when you see the wonderful advancements in knowledge and technology throughout the Muslim cultures around the world. I'm aware of the control these laws may appear to have, but the true interpretations, followed by the majority of Muslims, are those which Allah has instructed us to follow and do not limit our ability to expand our knowledge."

Jacob could relate to this, after all, Islam was not the only religion who sometimes tried to control faithfulness. When he was a boy, he was taught the Catholic Church and Jesus was the only way to God. It was a sin, punishable by a trip to Hell to believe otherwise.

Jacob wondered if the direction of the meeting was going

in the right direction. It seemed both of them were giving opinions instead of getting to the facts.

As if reading his mind, Muhja said; "Jacob, your confusion and skepticism of the laws of Islam, and other religions, is well noted. There are so many questions inherent within your observations I fear discussing them in such a broad format will not allow you to receive answers to any of your questions. I'd like to take a step back and ask that we address your questions one at a time so we don't miss anything."

"Excellent," Jacob quickly responded, and without a moments hesitation asked his first question.

"In my search for God, my confusion with religion has deepened. Each religion has multiple paths, all of which proclaim that the same God provided their unique scriptural foundation. With the vast differences in interpretations of the same scripture how is anyone supposed to know who is right? Why is this all so confusing, Muhja?"

"I understand the confusion you have in your heart," she said as she gave him a maternal smile and continued in a soft voice.

"The scriptures are the only true source of God's Word we have. Granted, there is a lot of confusion with so many interpretations, and all too often we spend so much time debating the differences, we lose focus on what they have in common."

"Actually, Muhja, as I think more about it how man interprets or misinterprets the scriptures is really the second part of my bewilderment."

"And what is the first?" Muhja asked.

"The first is why a loving and compassionate God would include such violence and brutality in the scriptures in the first place. I have read in many scriptures where God has obliterated entire civilizations to punish those who did not keep His Laws. Many of them ruthless laws which originated thousands of years ago, then passed down first through an oral tradition, or word of mouth, and then written in scriptures decades later. Ambiguous laws Muhja, which permitted men to interpret them differently."

"What is ambiguous to you Jacob is clear and acceptable to others. Some scholars believe Allah intended mankind to have the flexibility to interpret his Word, and adapt it to the dynamics of changing world."

"If that's true, then I guess I really am confused."

"Why is that?" She asked.

"Because I don't believe a loving God wants me to show the wrath and revenge He displayed in scriptures. It doesn't make sense to me that children or animals were sacrificed to feed God's ego, or obtain his blessing. Nor can I believe a benevolent God wants me, or others, to live in poverty, or remain in the same ancient way of life Moses did."

Muhja patiently waited for Jacob to continue.

"I know somewhere in my notes," he said; "if I can find them, are passages from scriptures that direct men to annihilate non-believers. Wait! I found a couple. For instance; "And the Lord said to Moses, take all the heads of the people, and hang them up before the Lord against the Sun." (Num 25:4.9)

"Here's another!" he continued excitedly as though it was

new news to Muhja. "This one is from the Book of Joshua; "And Joshua's army killed everyone in Jericho, both men and women, young and old, oxen, sheep, and donkeys ...Joshua defeated the whole land ... he left no one remaining, but utterly destroyed all that breathed, as the Lord God of Israel commanded." (Joshua, 6:21 and 10:40)

"And in the Quran," Jacob went on without pausing, "There are similar instructions about killing and defeating Islam's enemies; "But as for those who disbelieve, garments of fire will be cut out for them; boiling fluid will be poured down on their heads." (Quran, 22.019)

"More confusing to me," he continued, "is that throughout these atrocities God is said to reward individuals and armies who die as martyrs; "On couches with linings of brocade shall they recline, and therein shall be the damsels with retiring glances, who no man or jinn hath touched before them." (Sura 55:56)

"Can you explain to me why a loving God would command one group of his people to murder helpless others, and then reward the killers with pleasure in Paradise? Is killing required? If I don't kill people who worship differently does that mean I don't love God or that God won't allow me to enter Heaven?"

"Muhja, how can God be so cruel, and expect unconditional love in return?"

"You have a lot of questions and doubts Jacob. Unfortunately, I am only a scholar, a person who validates her position based on the scriptures you struggle to understand. I can only explain the reasons for events of the past through scripture, and man's interpretation of how God wishes us to live. Though we can confirm that wars happened and certain people existed, there's nothing empirical outside our scriptures to explain Allah's reasons for what He does."

"Even if I was a prophet, Jacob, Allah may not deem it necessary to explain to me His reasons for doing things or allowing events to happen. I can interpret the Word of God as given to us in the scriptures, but I cannot read His mind. Because you don't have faith in the scriptures, the only answers you'll ever be satisfied with are those directly answered by God."

"You're right," Jacobs said. "But until I speak to God, how do I know which scriptures have been interpreted correctly and not changed?"

Muhja smiled. "I can tell you why I believe Allah's Word is accurate in the Quran, Sunnahs, and are enacted in the Community and Schools of Law, but I cannot, however, explain why Allah's Word in the Qu'ran conflicts with your expectations of how His laws and commandments should be."

"Fair enough," Jacob responded, "but tell me why Muslims believe the Islamic scriptures are absolute, and not those of Christianity or Judaism? For that matter, why is the Path of the Sunni the right path to God, instead of the Path of Shi'a, or one of the other Islamic paths? Who is right, Muhja? Which road do I take? I have traveled so far, yet I'm still lost! Do you know what I mean?"

"I will answer what I can, Jacob, but have patience in yourself, mankind, and Allah. First, as I told you earlier, we would eventually come back to the misconceptions of Islam. We have already come upon one that many people do not understand.

That is, Muslims, or should I say Islam, does not judge a person on the path or road they travel. Allah will make the final decision as to who will enter Paradise, not any man, prophet, or angel. As Muslims, we are taught to have tolerance for all religions."

"Tolerance for all religions? How is that, when sects like the Wahhabis spread messages around the world attempting to wipe out Judaism, Christianity and all other approaches to God?"

"Those are fundamentalists, Jacob. Pure Islam makes no claim to being the only road one can travel to reach God. We do believe, however, it is the only road a Muslim must travel. This, of course, differs from your travels on the Road of Christianity where total submission to Jesus is the only way."

"Do you mean Muslims don't submit themselves to Muhammad as Christians do to Jesus Christ?"

"No. Muslims believe in total submission only to Allah. We hold Muhammad, the final Prophet, in the highest regard, yet, we do not raise him or any of the other prophets, like Jesus or those found in your Bible, to the level of the divine. They were mortal men, messengers chosen by God to do God's work on earth."

"But wait," Jacob asked, "you say you don't worship Muhammad, yet after saying or writing his name Muslims always recite something which sounds like 'salla allahu wa sal. Isn't that a form of worship?"

"Absolutely not!" Muhja replied, grinning. "The phrase we use and the one you so eloquently butchered was 'salla allahu 'alaihi wa sallam,' which basically means 'peace be upon him."

This is an expression of the love and admiration we Muslims show to Allah's chosen prophet."

"Thanks for the clarification." Jacob replied, then immediately asked, "If you don't mind, I want to get back to your comment about Muhammad being the final prophet.

"This confuses me, because God has always used prophets, from Abraham to Moses, Jesus to Muhammad, to teach Man his word and laws. Why would he stop at Muhammad?"

"That's a good question," Muhja said; "please allow me to answer in sufficient detail so you understand how we know this is true."

"Foremost, Islam does not claim to be a 'new' religion. Instead, it is the continuation of the powerful messages from God first given to the Hebrew and Christian people. In the Quran, Christians and Jews are noted as the 'People of the Book,' meaning, of course, the Hebrew Bible and segments of the Christian New Testament. Islam reveres Jesus Christ for his love of the one true God, His teachings and the examples for man He set while spreading his messages of love and peace."

"Too bad nobody seems to follow them." Jacob interjected with a mild sneer.

"Nonetheless," she continued, "as I mentioned earlier, Islam doesn't believe any of Allah's prophets were divine. We never endeavored to become a new or separate religion. On the contrary, the Quran is a correction to Allah's messages in the original Hebrew scriptures. In the Quran, Allah tells Christians and Jews of his decision:

"People of the Book! Our Messenger (Muhammad) has come to you, making clear to you many things you have been concealing of the Book and forgiving you of much. A light has come to you from Allah and a glorious Book, with which He will guide whoever follows His pleasure in the way of peace, and brings them forth from darkness into the light by His will." (Quran 5:15-16)

"So then," Jacob asked, "Do Muslims find the Christian belief in Jesus Christ blasphemous?"

"There is a significant amount of contention between Christians and Muslims over the divinity of Christ. This isn't only because it took Christians hundreds of years to establish Jesus Christ as God in the collective imagination, but also because it contradicts the law Allah gave Moses in the Ten Commandments, thousands of years before, "Thou shalt have no other Gods before me."

"To answer your question, Jacob, Muslims for the most part believe the Christian interpretation of Jesus' divinity is blasphemy. We believe that Jesus was transformed from prophet, man, to God by early Christian clerics. Some Christian scholars also believe Jesus never claimed to be God, as indicated in this passage: "And Jesus said unto him, Why callest thou me good? There is none good but one, that is God." (Mark 10:18)

"Muslims are taught to believe only Allah will make the final determination of a person's acceptance into Paradise."

"Now, going back to where I left off, Islam is not a new religion, rather it's the final culmination of God's Word from the Hebrew scripture, or Old Testament, and the Gospels of the New

Testament. Now, let me explain how Islam began and why Muslims believe Muhammad is the last prophet of God.

"Around 600 years after the death of Jesus, and at the ripe old age of forty, Muhammad was summoned to Allah by the Angel Gabriel. Through Gabriel, Allah told Muhammad that He had given his original code of laws to the Jews through Moses and to Christians later, through Jesus Christ. However, after the death of His great prophets' mankind continued to deviate from His Word. To correct the deviations for the final time, Allah selected Muhammad, an honest and moral man, to be his final prophet and record His Word correctly in the Quran. Over a period of time Allah provided His Word to Muhammad who immediately dictated them word for word, therefore the Quran is infallible."

"Why was Muhammad Allah's last prophet, you asked? Since the Quran is the accurate restoration of Allah's' Word and final plan for mankind, there is no need for more prophets, nor is there anything more to teach man, because each word of the Quran is exactly how He gave it to Muhammad through the Angel Gabriel. The word of Allah in the Quran has remained the same for over 1400 years."

"But, Muhja," Jacob quickly responded, "Without exception, every religious path I've traveled, and every religious person I've spoken to, has told me a similar story. What makes the Quran and Islam different? And didn't Muhammad's recitation of the Quran then shut the door for future communication with God?"

"As a religious scholar I can appreciate your confusion. I, too, have been in your position. Nonetheless, I have explained to you why Muhammad is the last prophet. Let me clarify it was not

Muhammad who shut the door it was Allah. Now, let me focus on why the validity and infallibility of the Quran differs from other scriptures."

"Up to this point, I've spoken in general terms for all Muslims. The Quran to Muslim's is Allah's final word to mankind; period! Because every word in the Quran was recorded immediately and exactly as it was told to Muhammad, it differs from the manner in which other scriptures were written. The Quran wasn't written by men decades or centuries after the prophet's death. This helps us to validate the truthfulness of our scriptures."

Muhja's last statement got Jacob's attention. Yes, she has proof! He thought to himself. His journey may well end on the Road of Islam.

"Are you saying then," he asked, "that the Quran has remained unchanged for all of these years?"

"Two of the original Quran exist today. One is in Istanbul, and the other in Tashkent, Uzbekistan. There are no deviations between them; they are identical word for word."

"More spectacular is that during the last century scholars from the University of Munich collected over forty thousand copies of the Quran from different cultures and different periods of time. For over half a century they compared each of these manuscripts to the original two, and guess what?"

"They found no discrepancies!" Jacob responded.

"Absolutely none," Muhja proudly stated.

"That is fantastic," Jacob said; "and I don't want to appear a bull-headed pessimist, but even with the great care Islam has taken to preserve the Quran, like other scriptures individual words and phrases may have several meanings. The word ʿayn, for example, can mean an organ of sight, running water, gold, or spy. As a scholar, don't you have trouble determining which meaning is accurate? The problem I still have is that people interpret these things the way they want others to hear and follow them, without question."

For the first time, Jacob noticed that Muhja seemed displeased with him, as though she resented his doubts.

He continued, "I realize my comments sound like I don't believe any scriptures, but I am sincerely confused about who is right. I've never been able to verify that God has ever spoken to anyone."

"Jacob," she said, "earlier in our conversation I explained I would not have all the answers you are looking for. Your last question is one of those that neither I, nor anyone else besides Allah, will have the response you seek. I can't explain in any greater detail the extreme care that Muslim leaders have taken to ensure the final word of Allah is written in the Quran."

"Jacob, you aren't looking for knowledge, or suggestions regarding for the path you should travel, you're looking for proof, physical, untainted, and indisputable proof that God exists."

"Wanting to believe in God," she continued; "and believing in God are two very different things. The former is no more than a wish. In the absence of a 'one-on-one' sit-down conversation with God, why do you believe you will find the truth on any of the paths you will travel? Your comments and questions extend beyond an uncertainty about whether the word of God is accurate. If you don't believe in the scriptures, be they Christian, Jew, Muslim, or others, then most certainly your next question must be 'does God truly exist?"

"No!" Jacob interrupted. "I want to believe God exists." Jacob paused to reflect on his ambiguous answer. I think God exists, he said to himself. But what did he mean by "thinking" God exists? Before his journey he could have told someone he believed God existed, why was it hard to commit to that now? What changed? Was it the repeated contradictions that made it more difficult to commit to his beliefs, or that the answers were the same, regardless of the path he traveled?

Jacob wondered if he would ever find God and escape from his quandary. He thought of how easy it would be to stop trying to find God and commit to one religion, no questions asked. But what if he chose the wrong one?

"Are you sure your dilemma is only whether God's Word is correct?" Muhja asked, interrupting his thoughts.

"Yes… I mean, no," Jacob stammered. "Yes, I think God exists, but I'm not sure His word is accurate in any of the religious scriptures written by men."

"Personally," Muhja replied, "I would find it difficult to believe in God if I did not believe what those who have been in contact with God have told me through scripture."

"But you already said that the Gospels and Bible are incorrect. Doesn't that mean the teachings of Jesus, Moses and other prophets before Muhammad are invalid too? If those scriptures aren't true, then who has God been talking to?"

"That is not what I said, Jacob," Muhja sharply responded. "What I said was that many, not all, of the original laws of the Hebrew scriptures and the Gospels have been distorted through generations of human intervention, making it extremely difficult for anyone to determine what the truth is. The Quran, on the other hand, corrected the errors and returned the original law of Allah to all mankind."

"Jacob," she continued in a sincere tone, "You are on the threshold of resolving your faith. It is not so much now about finding God, but whether you believe in God. If you do, even if He doesn't jump up and greet you, then eventually you will select a path to travel which is most in line with the beliefs in your heart."

"The final counsel I will give you is from deep within my heart. On whichever road you decide to follow, do not expect it to be free of man-made potholes. Trust the goodness in yourself, and others. Someday you will make your decision, and tonight I believe you understand how I made mine. May Allah bless and guide you through the love in His heart." She rose from her chair and grasped Jacobs's hands.

"Thank you, Muhja, for your time, knowledge and compassion for me and my quest. And, thank you for being a friend. May our paths cross many times again, and Allah never leave your heart."

Muhja smiled lovingly, tapped Jacob's shoulder, turned and left the library.

Jacob woke before dawn to a melodious Muezzin's voice calling the Muslim faithful to Morning Prayer. As he watched the procession of believers entering the mosque he was deeply inspired by their adherence to the traditions of Islam and devotion to God. He knew Muslims around the world, regardless of their sect, would be facing east to Mecca, worshiping Allah, and giving thanks to the Prophet Muhammad.

As he watched the crowds he wondered how many of them prayed to God, or Allah, to thank Him for His love and blessings, and not merely to satisfy an ancient religious commandment. It was time to move on.

.

For many more absorbing and exhausting days Jacob traveled from one path of Islam to the next. On each he asked clerics and laymen questions similar to those he'd put to Muhja and the others. The responses he got varied from cordial to antagonistic.

As his travels on the Road of Islam drew to a close, a local tribal leader invited Jacob to stay at his home to rest. He spent the next few days at the oasis summarizing his observations and thoughts in his journal:

Upon leaving Muhja and the Path of the Sunni, I continued traveling until I came to the Path of the Shi'a, which is followed by about 15% of all Muslims. There I had the chance to speak to many Shi'a clerics in an effort to understand why they had separated from the Sunni, and why they believe their path is the one leading to God.

The Shi'a, as the Sunni, believe the Quran is Allah's final word and hold a devout love for the Prophet Muhammad. But, this common love for Allah and Muhammad is overshadowed by the hatred that festers between the two groups.

This hatred is rooted in the Shi'a belief that the succession of Muhammad, "his God given authority," passed down through Muhammad's family, beginning with his nephew, Ali. They do not believe caliphs selected by the community should govern Islam, as the Sunni do.

The disparity in methods for choosing a successor influences Islamic society, laws, religious ideology, and how Muslims live their day-to-day lives.

For example, the Shi'a believe Allah chooses an Imam through Muhammad's family succession. An Imam is not only the spiritual leader of the community or state, but is also the sole author of infallible Hadith's and other Muslim laws. I could not comprehend how a man's word is infallible, or he is void of all sin. To me, it gives a human God like powers to interpret scripture, justify wars, and maintain absolute power through implementation of strict laws. More confusing, there is more than one Iman, so who is right?

The more I learned the more I understood the scope of this schism. The Sunnis elect their caliphs from the community. They do not have to be descendants of Muhammad, and their

Hadiths are not infallible. Sunni caliphs are also thought capable of sin, unlike the imams of the Shi'a.

From the Path of Shi'a, I traveled several other paths crisscrossing the Road of Islam. Some were too small to mention, yet others were of particular interest, as the Path of the Sufi. Sufism integrates a belief in mysticism with Islam. Sufis believe personal experiences with Allah can be attained through self-discipline and meditation. Although this was not a large path, it has been influential in the development of many of the traditions that have built the foundations of Muslim communities.

After the Path of the Sufi, I spent a short time on the narrow Path of Wahhabi. I followed this path with a sense of apprehension, not knowing what to expect from the fundamentalist Wahhabi leaders or their followers. However, I was treated with suspicious kindness and was able to confirm what other Muslims had told me: Wahhabis are fundamentalists adamant in their belief that theirs is the only true Path of Islam, all other religions are false.

Wahhabis reject all luxuries, dancing, gambling, music, drugs, drinking and tobacco. This was especially surprising to me, since the lavish lifestyle of the Saudi royal family, who are said to be Wahhabis, is far from one of poverty or piety.

I have gained so much new knowledge about the similarities and differences found among Islam's sects. With this new insight, I feel I am better able to appreciate that a Muslim's commitment to Allah is as strong as a Christian's is to Jesus Christ.

I remain discouraged, however, that everyone seems to hold fast to their beliefs, while declaring all other faiths are wrong. To this end, I feel that, in spite of the thousands of miles I've traveled, I have hardly moved an inch. I can only hope God knows I remain committed to finding Him.

THE ROAD OF JUDAISM

Jacob knew the only way to triumph over his despair was to focus on the road ahead. All was not lost, he told himself; he still had the ancient Road of Judaism before him. This was where God chose Abraham as the first patriarch and sealed his new covenant with mankind.

But soon all hell broke loose. Abraham had two sons; Ishmael was his first son born by his wife Sara's hand maiden, Hager, an Egyptian; is the patriarch of Arabs or Islam. Isaac, born with Gods' blessing by the once infertile Sara, and later his son Jacob are the patriarchs of Judaism and Christianity.

Jacob frowned as he recalled the hatred and quests for power that had been played out here, long before Judaism, Christianity, and Islam had even developed into their present states. Isaac and Ishmael's feud for the promised lands has been going on for over 5000 years. No wonder there is so much hate here, he muttered to himself.

However, more important, Jacob said to himself, God was here! Maybe he never left?

As he began his journey down the Road of Judaism, Jacob was still struggling with Muhja's question: If you don't believe in the scriptures, be they Christian, Jew, Muslim, or others, then most certainly your next question must be 'does God truly exist?"

But what if Muhja was mistaken, and God is on one of the paths of religion, waiting for each of us to find Him? What if the reason people don't find God is because they give up their search too soon, as he had done before? What if people selected a religion for convenience, because looking elsewhere brought up too many complicated questions?

What if Muhja, gave up to soon? What if? What if? What if?

Many paths along the Roads of Christianity and Islam were intertwined with the same places located on the Road of Judaism. Jerusalem was a prefect example. There, each of the three groups had battled one another for ownership of the city for thousands of years. For the Jews, Jerusalem is the holiest city, King David's capital, and the home to Solomon's Temple. For Christians, it is the holy city where Jesus of Nazareth was crucified and resurrected. In Islam, it is the blessed city where Muhammad ascended to Paradise from the Dome of the Rock.

He recalled that the Jewish Bible, or Tanakh, includes the Torah, the prophets' teachings, and Rabbinical interpretations of the texts. He set off to find a rabbi to help him navigate the paths of Judaism.

When he asked those he met whom he should seek out for advice, a Rabbi Benjamin Golden was mentioned time and again. He was told the rabbi was a man of sincerity, progressive ideas, and always glad to help a traveler navigate the maze of Judaism.

Rabbi Golden exuded a frank friendliness, and was eager to help Jacob find the answers he sought, but he gave no guarantee he could introduce him to God. In fact, the portly rabbi volunteered to accompany Jacob on his journey across as many of the ancient Hebrew paths he wished. Jacob accepted his offer, and found the man's charisma and intellect lent invaluable credibility to Jacob and his quest.

"Rabbi Golden," Jacob asked; "the Road of Judaism is the most ancient of the three religions. Nevertheless, in the twenty-first century there are only about fourteen million Jews. Is it a lost religion?

Rabbi Golden replied, "Yes, the numbers are small, but still Judaism is not lost."

"Really?" Jacob asked.

"Yes, I'm sure." the rabbi responded. "Judaism isn't a religion that solicits new followers, but this doesn't mean our beliefs are wrong or others are correct. Converting to Judaism requires a total commitment by the individual. One cannot automatically become Jewish; it is only possible by birthright or after a lot of hard work. If your mother is Jewish, you are Jewish, but if not, then you must convert to Judaism."

"Generally speaking," he continued; "Jews do not try to convert others to Judaism. One reason is because we do not see a need to convert because God alone will decide who enters Heaven based on their actions in this life. You don't get a guaranteed piece of Heaven simply because you are a Jew."

Jacob was intrigued by the notion of putting the onus on the individual to be accountable for his actions.

"A person could become a Jew", Rabbi continued, "if they chose, but once they converted they must live their life by the laws of Judaism. If you don't like the rules, then don't join."

Jacob liked what he was hearing; maybe he would find God on this ancient Road.

"So Jacob, if you wish to convert to Judaism," the rabbi was saying, "you must complete a year of education about the Jewish religion and Halakhah, Jewish Law. Be prepared, by tradition you will be turned away from starting your formal education no fewer than three times over a several-month span."

"Upon completion of your education, you are brought before a rabbinical court, a Beit Din, for oral testing on these laws, including the 613 commandments you are agreeing to live by. If you pass, you are almost a Jew."

"What do you mean, 'almost a Jew'?" Jacob asked with surprise.

"Well, Jacob, if you've not been circumcised, and you wish to be a Jew, you must be."

"Ouch!" Jacob responded. He was glad his parents had already taken care of that for him.

"The good news, however, is that once you have completed these requirements, you are as much a Jew as anyone else. You see, Jacob, Judaism is not a list of traditions relating to God and the universe; it's a comprehensive way of life for those who are Jews."

"But isn't Judaism a race of people, as well as a religion? Jacob asked. He was feeling a bit confused.

"To someone who doesn't understand Judaism, what I'm about to say could confuse you more. However, if you let go of any preconceived opinions you may have, I think you'll find this interesting. Remember though, depending on the path of Judaism you travel, the message might differ. I am most always, speaking of the majority.

"I understand!" Jacob responded.

"Good," said Rabbi Golden as he continued, "First, we do not consider ourselves a 'race' of people, because, as I mentioned earlier, anyone can become a Jew through conversion . It doesn't not matter if you're black, white, Asian, Hispanic, or some other race; if you convert and are accepted, you are a Jew."

"But isn't that the same with Christianity, or Islam?" Jacob asked.

"That's my exact point; there is no race of Christians or Muslims, they come from many cultures and races. The same is true of Judaism."

"But Judaism is a religion?"

Rabbi Golden paused as he considered his answer. "That's an interesting question, Jacob," He replied, "and one that has a different answer depending on the path you travel. Let me explain it this way. Judaism is a religion as it pertains to a group of people believing in God and a set of His laws. But, if it was solely a religion, then I am afraid it we might be failing.

You see, there are many people who are Jews that do not believe in the religious aspects of Judaism. More than half the Jews in Israel classify themselves as 'secular,' and many don't believe in God at all. They remain Jews, however, and see Judaism as a culture of people who share similar traits, as in any family."

"So to clarify then, Rabbi," "you can be a Jew, but not believe in God?"

"Actually Jacob" Rabbi replied: "there are many Jews who don't believe God exists, yet they remain Jews and part of the Jewish family. I think your confusion comes from your Christian background. Should you decide not to believe that Jesus Christ is the Son of God, then you would no longer be a Christian. Islam works the same way. A Muslim must accept Muhammad as the final prophet, or they are not a Muslim. Do you see the distinction I am trying to make?"

"Yes. Thank you," Jacob replied.

"But, the world knows Judaism as only a religion, so let us leave it that way for now. However, Judaism has no formal set of beliefs that one must agree to follow to remain a Jew. While there is a place for belief, Jews focus more on their actions today, than on how to get into Heaven. We believe the way we live today will determine where we will be in the afterlife, but I'll get to that later."

"Unlike some religions, Judaism doesn't focus on abstract concepts, such as what God looks like or where Heaven and Hell are located. Yes, there are debates and disagreements between scholars regarding the nature of God, the afterlife, and even the universe, but there are no official edicts that people must follow."

"This seems like an open way of belief," Jacob commented, "but isn't there a list of basic beliefs that must be followed? I think it's called …."

"Rambam's Thirteen Principles of Faith," Rabbi Golden finished the sentence for him.

"Yes, that's it."

"You don't give yourself enough credit Jacob, there are many Jews who don't know of the list.

"Rambam's list is probably the closest anyone has come to listing a standard set of beliefs for Judaism. Nevertheless, there are still many topics of disagreement and debate. But the list," Rabbi said as he pulled a small card from his wallet, "demonstrates the simplicity of our beliefs, It says:

> God exists
> God is one and unique
> God is spiritual
> God is eternal
> Prayer is directed to God alone
> Words of the Prophets are true
> Moses' words and prophecies are true
> The written Torah and oral teachings in the Talmud
> were given to Moses
> There will be no other Torah
> God knows the thoughts and deeds of men
> God will reward the good and punish the bad
> The Messiah will come
> The dead will be resurrected

"They do appear simple, like the Ten Commandments," Jacob replied, "but aren't they still dissected, debated and followed through different interpretations?"

"Yes my friend, and 'debated' is an understatement!" the Rabbi chuckled.

"Rabbi, if I may interrupt?" Jacob asked.

"Absolutely."

"I'm very impressed with the openness and apparent flexibility of thought and beliefs you've told me about. I'm ashamed to admit that, except for reading several books and articles, I only have limited knowledge of Judaism. But, in addition to the things on that list, isn't there also a set of daily laws that provide instructions for every aspect of a Jew's life? Having laws by which people must live seems to contradict what you've' said about free will."

"Good observation," Rabbi Golden replied. "Let me answer as simply as I can. Jewish law, collectively, provides guidance to devout Jews for building their spiritual life and addresses what to eat and wear, how to worship God, how to treat other Jews and non-Jews, hygiene, prayers, and more."

"Jewish Law 'collectively'?" Jacob asked.

"Right. The Jewish law is collectively known as Halakhah, and consists of the Torah, Nevi'im, the teachings of the prophets, and the Ketuvim, or writings, which include various books of the Bible you know, such as the Psalms, Proverbs, Chronicles, and so forth."

Before Jacob could ask another question, Rabbi Golden continued. "As for the timing of our laws and traditions, you must remember that Judaism received God's laws before Christianity or Islam even existed. Had you begun your journey with Judaism, the origination point for scriptures and laws, the timeline of events and some of the other topics we discussed earlier might have been easier for you to understand."

"But Rabbi Golden," Jacob said, "regardless of which laws or scriptures were first, Judaism still has a comprehensive set of laws that govern the lives of its people. Why, if God gave man free will, must men adhere to laws written thousands of years after God's covenant with Abraham and Moses?

"And if God has given man the aptitude to reason, the desire to enhance wisdom, and the ability to make choices, why did He put laws in place which limit the growth of discovery, and establish parameters for questioning scripture and bondage to a specific ideology?"

Rabbi Golden smiled and replied, "Let me try to explain why God has provided a complete guide for mankind.

"For argument's sake, accept the events I mention as proven Biblical accounts, even though you may not agree with them in total. If you recall, God provided Adam and Eve with all the gifts you have indicated. What did they do? They lost their lease on Paradise."

"God gave mankind more chances for growth and to use free will through Noah, Abraham, Jacob, Isaac, Ishmael and others, long before the Prophets Jesus and Muhammad emerged. On each occasion, mankind screwed things up. So, if you were God Jacob, what would you do?"

Jacob knew he had been set up, but smiled and answered, "Write instructions for what had to be done."

"I rest my case!" Rabbi Golden crowed as a broad smile crossed his face.

Jacob grinned and put the question on hold, unanswered. He knew the rabbi had given him the short answer, and anyhow, he was looking for God, not wanting to debate what others believe. Yet, he didn't want to believe God limited man's creativity, curiosity, or abilities with a set of explicit laws. He smiled as he thought that God probably wonders why it has taken people so long to make the most of the wisdom He provided them.

"If I may," Rabbi asked, bringing Jacob back to the conversation, "let me continue with a bit more background on Jewish law and how it developed."

"Sure."

"The scriptures included in the laws of Judaism are found foremost in the Torah, the written word of God. The Talmud, or oral Torah, was brought forward through the centuries, verbatim, by scholars who memorized it in its entirety."

"Was this similar to how laws were carried forward in Christianity and Islam?" Jacob asked.

"Yes," Rabbi responded, "and as I understand from our initial conversations your concerned with the accuracy and authenticity of scriptures. You will be pleased to know many Jews feel the same way, and look to the Torah and other laws as guides that should be adaptable over time."

Jacob smiled as he thought to himself; Yes, maybe I am not alone after all?

"The Halakhah is the written law we are taught to obey. It

includes 613 mitzvot, or commandments, from the Torah. It also offers teaching and guidance from the prophets and rabbis who have the responsibility of interpreting scripture."

"613 commandments? I thought there were only ten?"

"Yes!" Rabbi responded laughing, "you have a lot of catching up to do."

"You've got that right, but what are they all about?"

"Of the 613 there, are 248 that describe the rewards from God for obeying His laws and 365 punishments for disobeying them."

"So they stress God's wrath, more than His kindness?" Jacob asked.

"Actually, it's about even, since 24 of the commandments focus on avoiding forbidden sexual relations, ranging from incest to sodomy and to sex with beasts."

"Or your third cousin eight times removed." Jacob said lightheartedly.

"Other commandments," Rabbi continued, paying no heed to Jacob's last comment, "cover everything from marriage and divorce to business transactions, prayers, the treatment of Jews and non-Jews, and more."

As he listened, Jacob noted how similar the stories of origin and establishing laws were across each Road of religion. He wondered to himself, if this might be the one aspect all three religions agree on?

"Rabbi," Jacob asked; "are the Jews God's chosen people?"

Rabbi Golden smiled; "I hope so, Jacob." He replied jovially, than continued. "Seriously, my friend, Jews, and remember we are speaking of the majority of Jews," Rabbi emphasized, "don't believe they are more special to God than Christians, Muslims or others. I laugh each time I respond to this question because most people do not know the story which states that Yahweh --,"

"You mean God?" Jacob interrupted.

"Yes." Rabbi Golden replied and continued, "Yahweh offered the Torah to the Jews last of all peoples, and basically threatened them into accepting it. They eventually did, but it came with a big responsibility. For instance, as a Christian, you adhere to Ten Commandments, while we obey 613. No, Jacob, we do not believe we are God's 'chosen people,' or are first in line to Heaven."

"Nevertheless, as Jews we do believe we were chosen by God to teach all people His laws, as they were given to us in His covenant with Abraham. I believe this has created some of the schism with other religions and peoples of the world, as 'chosen' was interpreted to mean the Jewish people thought they had more rights to God. It's not so, not at all." Rabbi concluded in a somber voice.

"Thank you, Rabbi Golden," Jacob said sincerely as he recognized the sadness Rabbi felt for this misunderstanding.

"Heaven," Jacob said, moving the rabbi to another topic, "What is Judaism's position on Heaven and the afterlife?"

"Whew!" Rabbi Golden said laughing. "That was quite a

transition, from the chosen people, to Heaven and the afterlife!"

Jacob smiled as Golden continued. "Let me see, Heaven and the afterlife, Olam Ha-Ba."

"Olam what?"

"Olam Ha-Ba is our view of the afterlife. Because Judaism is focused on life here and now, there's not a great deal of scripture on the afterlife, and so we are left with a great deal of room for personal views. The Torah and Talmud both focus on life on earth and each person's requirements to fulfill our duties to God and fellow men.

The spiritual afterlife we refer to as Olam Ha-Ba is 'the world to come.' Christians and traditional Jews call it Heaven, while Muslims refer to it as 'Paradise.' Nevertheless, to each of us it is the place where we will be rewarded as a result of our adherence to God's commandments in proportion to the way we lived by His laws in this life."

"In proportion to the number of the 613 mitzvots, that is commandments you abide by?" Jacob asked.

"Jacob, I enjoy your cross-examination style of questioning me!" Rabbi Golden said.

"I'm not sure what you mean?"

"The way in which you ask the same question more than once and within different contexts to confirm or disprove previous answers," the rabbi explained.

"Honest, Rabbi Golden," Jacob said apologetically, "I never intended to trap you, it's just an old habit of mine from years of jury trials. I guess I was seeing if God's rewards were dependent on how strictly you followed his rules. "

Rabbi Golden chuckled as he assured Jacob he wasn't offended, just intrigued

"As I said, most Jews believe the ancient texts are a guide, not an absolute set of inflexible laws, established by God for His people. As mankind continues to advance and societies change, so must God's guide. It is very hard for many of us to believe God wanted us to remain in sandals, living off goat milk and sleeping in tents. No, Jacob, it's not the number of mitzvots we perform daily that will bring us rewards in the world to come, it's the way we lived and treated others in this life."

"Thank you for explaining a little about Olam Ha-Ba, but how do you believe it will come to be?"

"That, my friend, will happen when we enter the Messianic Age, or the end of the world as we know it today."

"You mean the end of the world as St. John described it Revelation?" Jacob asked.

"Not exactly. It's a time when the Moshiach, or Messiah, will come and return the one God of Abraham to all the peoples of the world.

"As you know, Jews don't believe Jesus was the Messiah. Traditional Jews believe the Moshiach will not be divine or our savior. These characteristics are Christian-based and not recorded anywhere in the Torah. Nonetheless, we do believe he will be a great political and military leader descended from King David who will redeem the Jewish people and restore peace under the one God of Abraham."

"Do you believe this will happen?"

"Yes, because I believe God is, and if God is, then the rest of the basic laws we were provided must also exist."

Jacob understood the rabbi's position and didn't intend to debate his beliefs. After all, no one had proof. Changing the topic, Jacob asked,

"Why have Jews been hated and persecuted by countries, religions, and governments since the time of Abraham and Jacob?"

"That's a question we've been trying to answer since that time," Rabbi Golden replied in a slightly frustrated tone. "We have assumed," he continued, "it pertains to several factors, such as the confusion over the term 'God's chosen people.' Another reason is the misconception that Jews control the world's economic and financial powers. Even in 17th century and after, Jews in Russia and Poland were dirt poor but still hated for these reasons."

"It was also proclaimed," he continued; "the Jews killed Jesus and, though we were exonerated during the Second Vatican Council in 1963, we are still targeted because of this hateful lie. Toss in racial theory, territorial disputes and us being a small group easily beaten upon, and you have a bitter recipe for anti-Semitism."

"Rabbi, you have taught me a great deal, and I appreciate your friendship, however, I must go now to find God. Will I meet God on one of the paths of Judaism we have yet to travel?"

"Will you find God on paths you have yet to travel?" the Rabbi repeated. "If you mean the physical God you so desperately seek Jacob, the answer is no. Unless of course, God decides to manifest himself to you. It is God alone, Jacob, who is all-powerful and all-knowing and who will decide when you will see Him."

"If God is truly all-powerful and all-knowing, that would mean He knows when an accident, natural disaster or evil scheme by men, like genocide, is going to happen. Why does He choose not to stop it?"

The rabbi answered, "Your question is well beyond my aptitude to answer. I believe God is all-knowing, and could show you scripture to prove my belief, but I know that would not satisfy you. Unfortunately, Jacob, beyond what I have told you, I can't explain why God acts as He does."

Jacob appreciated that Rabbi Golden hadn't responded with the old adage "God works in mysterious ways," the catch-all phrase used in religion to hide the fact people don't have all the answers. Jacob often wondered if he were omnipotent and omniscient, as God, if he would have watched the car slam into Jessica without saving her, or be able to watch a child being raped, die of starvation or disease and yet not provide food or medicine.

Rabbi Golden knew his answer did not satisfy Jacob, but he had nothing more to say except; "Jacob, you have traveled many roads of religion, but you have not found God, in a bodily sense, that is. I'm not sure it will be different on the paths left for you to travel. I can only explain to you what other Jews and I have chosen to believe without requiring proof from God."

"Our belief is simple Jacob, we accept God exists, and no proof is required. Further, we believe in the basic teachings of the Torah: there is only one God, and He or She created everything in the universe. I say "He or She" because we don't spend time trying to define God. We believe God transcends all time, is always around us, and knows all things past, present and future, including when the Moshiach will be born. God is merciful, just and eternal."

"Blind faith?" Jacob said in a soft voice, not intending the rabbi to hear him.

"It has been called worse things, Jacob. But, if accepting God is 'blind faith,' then I guess we are guilty."

"We still have several roads to travel; you don't need to make a decision right now. Give yourself time to absorb the knowledge you have obtained, and then focus on your decision. Most important, allow God time to reconcile the troubles within your heart."

Even though it was said to be the first Road chosen by God, the Road of Judaism, like the Roads of Christianity and Islam, included many divergent paths. Each meandered into the distance, confident that it alone led to the true interpretation of God's word.

As Jacob traveled with Rabbi Golden across the paths of Orthodox, Ultra, Reformed, Conservative, Zionist and Reconstructionist Jews, he was appreciative of the new knowledge of Judaism he had gained, but saddened by the commonality with other paths he had followed. Here, too, there was no proof of God's presence, yet everyone claimed to be following God instructions.

In spite of his concern that God had not yet appeared to him, Jacob found his time on the paths of Judaism valuable.

He learned that Jews are typically more tolerant to other religions. As a result, it seemed they attracted many other spiritual travelers not associated with Judaism, Christianity or Islam. Many were concerned with seeking new perspectives of God and the universe as they sought to reach a higher level of spirituality. Others were looking for knowledge to compare faiths, while some traveled to validate their personal beliefs.

Jacob valued the conversations he and Rabbi Golden had with the other spiritual travelers they had met. Travelers from philosophies as Buddhism, Shintoism, Pranayama and more, gave great intellectual stimulation, yet also triggered a sense of mild despair as he recognized the number of paths a seeker looking for God could travel in search of Him.

But why? He asked himself. Why would God create so many paths of religion? Is it so we could not find Him? On the other hand, did God allow the maze of religion because it does not matter which path a person chooses?

Maybe the rabbi had been right when he said God gave man free will, and that the confusion in our world is the result of the decisions we have made? What is true? Why was it still all so confusing? Where is God? These questions and more plagued him until he finally fell into a sound sleep.

The next morning, aware their time together was reaching

its end, Jacob met Rabbi Golden and embraced him in a gesture of sincere friendship and thanked the him for the help he provided to a lost stranger.

"It was my pleasure, Jacob," the rabbi replied; "foremost I am thankful for the opportunity God has given me to befriend you. But close behind is my appreciation to you for allowing me to rekindle my faith through your eyes."

"Rekindle, but you're a Rabbi!"

"Deep down inside Jacob, I think you want to be a Jew," Golden answered with a broad smile on his face.

"In all seriousness my friend, even those of us who practice our faith diligently have doubts at times. Being a part of your quest has allowed me to build on the strength of my commitment to God, and the path of Judaism I have chosen. Through our dialogue with other rabbis, I have learned the faith in their heart is real and regardless of how it may differ from the path I follow it is the one they have chosen to live by."

"You have helped me more than you can imagine, Jacob Hinsen, and the only way I feel I can repay you is to offer my sincere counsel."

"Thank you," Jacob answered.

"What I have to say is not based on my religious preference; it's what I feel in my heart as a man, one who believes in God and recognizes the pain you hold in your heart. I can tell, Jacob, that you carry a pain that is deeper than the questions we've discussed during our journey."

Sadness overcame Jacob as he thought of Jessica. He debated telling Golden about her, but decided to keep it to himself to ensure his focus remained on finding God.

Rabbi Golden saw the sadness in Jacob's eyes and knew he had been right.

"Jacob, as your friend, I know you've traveled a long way and on many paths of religion, yet this has only added to your confusion, instead of providing the definitive answers you seek. But, confusion is a component of the world we live in. Yet, in many cases we are able to work through our challenges to find an acceptable solution. The solution may not be exactly as we wanted, but we do have the ability to affect our outcomes.

"However, God and religion Jacob, offer a whole new challenge for those like you who remain undecided. You are frustrated because you do not have control of your situation. God has control, a God you try but cannot define, one with whom you cannot establish physical contact, one who will not provide you with personal answers or the proof you seek of His existence.

"Therefore, you live with the agony of uncertainty tearing at your heart. More frightening to you Jacob is that your decision will be based on having no proof of God in hand. You are afraid of the faith you must accept, which is required of any religion, or spiritual path."

"But why must I decide, why can't God manifest Himself and eliminate this dilemma?" Jacob asked forcefully, agitated once again by the realization he was back to having to decide what God wanted him to do.

Golden registered Jacob's sudden tension and placed his arm around him saying, "I have no answer for you, Jacob, except by giving us free will, God has decided that we, meaning the human race, must resolve our problems by growing closer to Him through our actions. We already have amassed technology that extends a person's lifetime; maybe God has also left it in our hands to bring about the spiritual transcendence needed after the centuries of hatred we created since He formed His covenant with Abraham."

"I'm also sorry that I do not have the proof you seek," Rabbi Golden continued, "and I regret that God didn't believe your situation so grave that it warranted His personal appearance. But for all we know, you may not have recognized God if He did appear."

"All I can say my friend is at this point in your journey you must trust in the information God has given you during your marvelous journey to purge your pain. You are a good man Jacob, do not neglect to search deep within yourself for answers."

The men bid each other farewell before Rabbi Golden returned to the long road, where their journey had begun.

As he watched him go, Jacob understood that, regardless of how complex or contradictory the world's religions seemed, there are countless wonderful people like Rabbi Golden, Muhja, Father Doyle, and others who endeavor to bring forth the compassionate and merciful teachings of God.

Jacob thanked God for this insight. He had been drawn to the chaos of religion for so long that he had lost focus on those who not only believe in God, but apply His message of love to their daily lives. These are the people who should be the leaders of religions, he thought to himself.

Jacob turned to leave the Path of Judaism and make his way home. As he traveled, his mind was flooded with the opposing views he encountered on his journey. But too, he recalled the magnificent places he had visited, the knowledge he acquired, the new ways of thinking he discovered, and the amazing people who had helped him in his struggle to find God.

Nevertheless, he remained troubled by the fact he had not found proof of God's existence; or confirmation which path God wanted him to follow. Without a sign or confirmation from God, how would he ever know if Jessica is at peace with the Lord? How would he ever know if he would be with her again?

JUDGMENT

For several months after returning home, I devoted myself to scrutinizing my notes and journals to ensure I remembered the precise answers to my questions and the spirit of the individual who had answered them. No memo, observation, obscure remark, pamphlet, symbol or image was ignored.

Reluctantly, I forced myself to probe the dark corners of my mind to recall memories I had given up for lost or deliberately suppressed; such as the carnage of war, eternally entrenched in a nineteen year olds mind. I re-examined my core beliefs by calling to mind events in my life to question whether I could prove God had saved me, or as Arnold alluded to me; saved by happenstance in a world of chaos

It was vital that I be unconditionally truthful to myself, regardless of where my judgments lead me. If I failed to do so, my long journey would be meaningless.

I sat at my desk, and removed my tattered journal and sorted notes from the drawer. As I collected my thoughts, I turned to a blank page in my journal to record my personal judgments, and beliefs.

Journal: October 6th

My journey across the Kingdom of Religious Confusion was full of twists and turns, more than anyone should have to experience in their search for God. In fact, the bias, hate and contradictions within and between religions often caused me to doubt God's existence. They certainly did little to confirm His presence in their worlds.

Equally disturbing was the sheer number of travelers I encountered who were also looking for God. I continue to wonder why God is so difficult to find. I do not take solace to know I am not alone in my search for Him.

Nonetheless, it was far from a journey of despair. It was a compilation of new insights, new friendships with self-sacrificing people who clarified their beliefs and spiritual passages to God. Individuals who opened their hearts to bestow the love they believed God expects each of us to share.

The details of my journey are told. The following entries document the rationale for the decisions I have made. Most importantly, I accept the foundation for my judgments are based on speculation. As in religion, paths of spirituality, or secular philosophies they will not be proven empirically during this life. As well, it is not my intent to propose differing beliefs are flawed.

As noted in the details of my journey, I did not find God in the flesh. Initially I slipped into depression after I returned, and thought it might be easiest to believe God did not exist, or accept any religion and become part of a group, and then hope their philosophy was genuine.

Yet, for reasons unknown to me, I was unable to accept either option. Sure, God remained unseen and did not send an angel to guide me, but I felt an essence within me encouraging me to go on. I cannot define the essence, and I am sure some would define it as dreaming, but I am confident I was never alone.

Let me stress, however, my decisions did not come about because of a "tingle" in my heart. Instead, I passed through many phases of reconciliation, soul searching and inner debate, until I discovered and accepted those observations and judgments most powerful in the transformation of my beliefs.

Extremely difficult for me, is the realization I cannot define God, or able to accept the theory God succumbs to human form, and behavior. Such as, taking sides between religions, or loving a Jew more than a Christian or Muslim. Or, confusing humankind with an array of images of His being, and contradicting theologies of His Word.

Although there are many definitions of God, no one religion can emperically prove their doctine is correct. Nor, can the speculation of atheists' prove religions are wrong. Therefore, the only way for me to accept a God who is not observable or readily assessable is through faith alone. This means the existence and essence of God is based on what I choose to believe as an individual.

Therefore, I have chosen to believe there is a God. Even

though the term "God" limits His scope to what I can comprehend. I believe there is an essence far more advanced than me, an essence I will continue to call God.

I believe the essence of God encompasses all things in the universe and beyond. How God works, where He or She resides, whether God is within me or outside of me, I cannot explain. Maybe the only proof is as Muhja, Father Doyle, Rabbi Golden and others have told me: the feeling must be based on an acceptance deep in my heart.

I have chosen not to believe the essence of God descended to earth in the form of a man in a secluded sector of the world to serve a small group of people. Because of my Christian upbringing, this was not an easy decision. I have chosen to believe Jesus as a conduit of a greater spirit, a prophet, as some have called him.

Given that I have chosen to believe in the essence of God, I had to decide upon the path I would follow to reach Him. At first, I felt my options were limited: religion or individual spiritual growth, a combination of both, or neither.

As I pondered my dilemma, I took into consideration why many people are comfortable within organized religion. It defines their connection to God. It provides a spiritual ideology, and format on how to live. They are confident that if they adhere to the rituals of their faith, God will grant them entrance into the afterlife.

I am no longer satisfied, however, within the confines of religion's restrictions and binding provisions, which I must accept in order to reach God. It is within these segregated groups where hatred has been nutured since the time of Abraham. By requiring stringent acceptance to an ideology, fostering an "us against you" mentality, and propagating fear from a vengeful God, religion has unbalanced God's message of love and free will, with man's implementation of rituals, sacrifices, punishments and control.

I choose to believe any ideology that proliferates; violence, hatred, supremacy, infallibility, or commands individuals to adhere to ancient rituals, is an ideology designed by men, and not by a loving God.

I believe I have been given "free will" to rationalize, make decisions, fail and try again until I have ascended to higher levels of spirituality.

I do not believe any religion or ideology owns God, or has empirical proof of His image or qualities. Nor, do I believe that non-believers possess any greater knowledge of what happens in the universe, or afterlife, with their speculative secular theories.

I believe religion and secular beliefs are not all controlling, when they share principles of love, and contribute significantly to helping the less fortunate.

I have chosen not to follow the path of any single religion or road of spirituality because I do not believe there is one with a direct link to the spirit of God. Right or wrong, I believe the message God wants me to align myself to is; "love God, and thy neighbor." I have decided to follow all paths that teach only the goodness of God.

There are many paths of spirituality without religious prejudices to travel. The Path of Pranayama, for example, encourages followers to question and uncover not only better answers to spiritual questions, but also better questions to comprehend the essence of God.

Many paths I will revisit, as the Path of Mormon. At first, Abby's comments regarding our ability to ascend to the spiritual essence of God made me doubt her's was a path God would want me to follow. Nevertheless, the concept intrigued me the more I thought about it. Although I may not become a god, aspiring to the essence of how I believe God wants us to be will help me transcend to a higher spiritual level.

As for my belief in an afterlife, I have decided to believe there is eternal life; call it Heaven, Paradise, reincarnation, or any other name. I am sure part of my decision is based on my hope there is more to our existence than life on earth. If not, I may never be with Jessica again, or continue to believe she is in a place of beauty, peace and love. It is my hope that my commitment to spiritual growth, without boundaries, will allow me to reside with God and Jessica when I have departed this life.

I do not think my beliefs will remain stagnant. Instead, they will adapt to new knowledge as I observe, question and absorb all teachings of goodness, the universe, and myself in my quest to reach a higher level of spirituality. I can only hope it is acceptable to the essence I continue to recognize and refer to as God.

If, however, I have chosen the incorrect paths to follow, I believe a loving God knows the chaos I am trying to reconcile, and the ease in which a seeker can lose their way. I believe if I should travel the wrong path, God will know my journey has been in a righteous direction, not perfect by a long shot, and accept me for trying.

Of course, should I find He is a God of wrath, jealousy and vengeance who requires strict adherence to the contradicting ancient laws of religion, then I am not sure it will matter if I reach Heaven, because it will seem like Hell to me.

Last, while I acknowledge the beliefs I have chosen are based on speculation, they have allowed me to remove the yoke of religious dogma without fear of God's reprisal. They have also reinforced my conviction that reaching God is a journey, a personal spiritual progression. Where the journey will end, transcends that which my human mind is capable of comprehending.